THE LAWYER DISDAINED IT.
THE PSYCHOLOGIST SWORE
IT COULDN'T HAPPEN.
AND THEY WERE WRONG . . .

"Regina! What's wrong with you?" Janet shook
her by the shoulders. Regina was slumped on
the floor, propped up by the wall, her eyes
open but blank.

She was slipping away, slipping away from the
hands, toward a void. She yearned to be there,
to be alone, forever out of reach, beyond
everything, to be nothing . . .

Not her! Janet thought. *He can't want her—
she's too pretty, like Viola; he knows he can't
trust her! He always hated women like her!*

But Janet felt it too. The whole house was alive
with it, alive with *his* death, resonating with his
sinister will and trembling with . . .

A SENSE OF SHADOW

Books by Kate Wilhelm

City of Cain
The Clewiston Test
Fault Lines
Juniper Time
Margaret and I
A Sense of Shadow
Where Late the Sweet Birds Sang

Published by TIMESCAPE BOOKS

Most Timescape Books are available at special quantity discounts for bulk purchases for sales promotions, premiums or fund raising. Special books or book excerpts can also be created to fit specific needs.

For details write or telephone the office of the Vice President of Special Markets, Pocket Books, 1230 Avenue of the Americas, New York, New York 10020. (212) 245-6400, ext. 1760.

A SENSE OF SHADOW

KATE WILHELM

A TIMESCAPE BOOK
PUBLISHED BY POCKET BOOKS NEW YORK

for Jennifer

A Timescape Book published by
POCKET BOOKS, a Simon & Schuster division of
GULF & WESTERN CORPORATION
1230 Avenue of the Americas, New York, N.Y. 10020

ISBN: 0-671-44116-7

First Timescape Books printing August, 1982

10 9 8 7 6 5 4 3 2 1

POCKET and colophon are trademarks of Simon & Schuster.

Use of the trademark TIMESCAPE is by exclusive license
from Gregory Benford, the trademark owner.

Printed in the U.S.A.

Part One

October 14

I FORGOT TO bring my journal with us. It's the first time in ten years that I haven't had it wherever I've happened to be. Lucas opened a chest of drawers and found one of his old school notebooks and handed it to me. Nothing in his room had been changed, he said, as though offended.

Our room, his old room, is very large. All the rooms in his father's house are large and airy. This one has twin beds, two chests, two comfortable chairs, a desk with its own chair, a long bookcase, and a radio and clock on the bedstand between the beds. There is plenty of room to move around the furniture, to get to the windows, to the closet, without being crowded. The windows are very tall, without curtains; they have heavy blue draw drapes. The bedspreads match the drapes. A boy's room, curiously lacking a trace of boyishness. I looked at the carpet—rust colored, fluffy, thick, and soft—to see if there was an old stain from a spilled cup of cocoa, paints, anything. There was nothing. Hotel room keeps coming to mind; this, the hotel where Lucas spent his childhood. There is no way to compare this to our cluttered apartment, two rooms heaped with our possessions. Much of the disarray is my fault, but Lucas contributed substantially to the mess. He was not messy when he was a child in his father's house. Also he did not collect anything—no fish, fossils, rocks, posters . . .

Lucas has gone out to walk with his brother Mallory. I watched them from our window: Lucas, slight and long haired, still thin from his bout with the flu last month; Mallory, forty pounds heavier, several inches taller, bear-like.

"We're all different," Lucas warned me. "Three brothers, all different in every way, and a sister like none of them. Same father, three different mothers. I come from a screwed up family, honey. Screwed up, screwed over."

This morning when his father's fourth wife called to tell Lucas his father was dying, he took a deep breath and said, "Finally."

"He isn't dead yet," Mallory said, when he met us at the airport. "But any time now." He clasped my hand, and studied my face for what seemed too long, then turned to Lucas. "Did he pay your way out?"

"Yes. We couldn't have come otherwise."

"Thought so. You talk to Greta?"

Lucas nodded. "I think she had a statement she was reading from. It didn't sound natural. Something about the will, and his demand that we all be here now."

"He didn't object that you brought Ginny?"

I was startled at his nickname for me. No one had called me Ginny since my grandfather died when I was very young. Any reservations I had about Mallory vanished at that moment. Lucas had described him, not the way he looked so much as the way he was: blunt, big and gentle, smart. He was sixteen years older than Lucas, and had been more father than brother to him. When Lucas was ten, his mother had died; Mallory had taken care of him for almost two years. I had been prepared to be jealous of Mallory, but there was no need.

Lucas said with some surprise that Greta had ordered two tickets for us, apparently expecting me to come along.

Mallory looked puzzled, then shrugged. "He made it clear that he didn't want Sarah here. And the kids were out. Curious." We started to walk toward the baggage claim area at the Portland airport, and he added, "Course, no way on this earth would Sarah have come."

Mallory drove us out to the farm, a little over an hour from the airport. When we left the highway for a private road of crushed red lava, Mallory said, "Old homestead starts right here, Ginny. Far as you can see."

We crossed a railroad line, then a bridge that spanned a rapid little river. To our left were fields of winter wheat, and other fields freshly plowed, ready to be planted. To the right were orchards, where some men were setting up a net under an apple tree, while a mammoth red machine reached for the trunk with a monstrous arm. Next was a pasture with a large pond and grazing cattle. Ahead were grassy hills and sheep, and there were higher hills, or mountains, deeply wooded.

I kept thinking, oh, my God! Lucas had said he grew up on a farm in Oregon, but there had not been even the slightest hint that he was talking about a plantation, land holdings that royalty might envy.

We turned on to a drive lined with rhododendrons, each standing alone. Beyond them the lawn flashed by in strobe-like glimpses of brilliant green, smooth enough to look artificial. The house looked small at first, but only because the evergreen trees around it were so tall. There were spruces and firs, a scattering of dogwood trees on one side of the house, deep borders of hedges and flowering bushes, chrysanthemums and dahlias in bloom, and a rose garden.

The exterior of the house is cedar, the first-story boards are vertical and others, on the upper floors, diagonal, meeting in the center, following the peak of the cedar-shake roof. Orford cedar, Mallory said, so rare now that it is hardly used for anything but decorative trim.

Mr. Culbertson had the living room added to the house before Lucas was born. The addition is wood and glass with a fieldstone fireplace. Curved stairs lead to an upper level where a balcony room overlooks the living room. The balcony has glass walls on the west and south. It is a room of plants, a hanging garden. Emerald greens, forest greens, pale shades of avocado . . . The light coming through the greenery into the living room below is cool and invigorating. It is like being in a deep forest.

All so lovely, I thought when I first saw the grounds, the house, the living room. It was too lovely to touch. Entering the living room, I felt almost as though we had been brought there to be stage props, that we were supposed to arrange ourselves here and there and never move again. I had a momentary vision of myself in a group of children being herded through a museum where nothing lived and the air was thick with warnings: Don't touch! Don't touch! All I retained of that field trip was the oppressive memory of hostile eyes watching. I had the same urge I had felt on that day, the urge to draw myself up as tightly as possible, to wrap my arms around myself, and concentrate on walking in order not to brush against anything, not to touch.

When we arrived, Conrad, the second oldest of the Culbertson sons, was in the living room with Janet, their sister.

Conrad is very tall and lanky. His arms and legs are almost abnormally long, and his feet are fascinating, the largest feet I've ever seen. He must have his shoes made for him. They look very comfortable and handsome, and surely there are few men who could wear them or who could pay for them. Conrad is forty, Mallory forty-six, Janet thirty-five. Lucas is thirty.

Janet and Conrad were having a drink at a black and chrome bar. She grinned at us and said, "We have gin, bourbon, and rye. No mixer, or soda. Father never did like to dilute liquor and, by God, in his house, no one else does either." She smiled at me and said, "Welcome to the family." And she hugged and kissed Lucas. Conrad hugged him, shook my hand.

Janet is obese; flab hangs down from her arms and under her chins. Her legs are monstrous. She wore a tentlike dress, a print with clusters of grapes climbing up ladders. She had on white ankle socks and no shoes.

She could be very pretty, I decided, trying not to stare at her. Her eyes are beautiful. They are as soft as a doe's eyes, very large, with heavy black lashes that sweep up in a curl. Her hands are pretty too. Her fingers, as boneless as Mona Lisa's, are long and pale with perfectly shaped nails. She could model rings or gloves, or eye makeup, or glasses. This in spite of the fact that she must weigh over a hundred pounds too much. If she were slimmer, how beautiful she would be, I kept thinking, sipping bourbon and water.

"We're all crazy, you know," she said, refilling her glass after handing drinks to Mallory and Lucas, pausing to look at me directly. "Crazy, but not dangerous. Amiably crazy. We're here to celebrate a death, you see, and since we're not really ghouls, we must be crazy."

"Shut up," Conrad said, but without inflection, as if he actually paid no attention to her.

They talked about the last half dozen or more years, bringing each other up to date, and it was pleasant and comforting to be in a family. I had always imagined a reunion would be something like this, taking turns at filling in the blanks after the separation that followed growing up, leaving home to pursue different ambitions.

Conrad was in charge of a laboratory of a chemical company based in Denver. He was the best dressed of them all, with gray slacks, a sport coat that must have cost him several hundred dollars, a dove-gray shirt that looked very much like silk. He was aloof, bored possibly, as if he had other, more pressing, matters on his mind and this was an irksome interruption that had to be tolerated with as good grace as he could manage.

Janet talked about her house, left to her by her grandmother. Seven years ago she had remodeled it, and now rented out three apartments, keeping the last for herself. What she needed, she said, was a maintenance robot, a creature she could store in a closet until needed, which was only every single day. With a glint of amusement in her eyes she told about fixing a plumbing leak herself when the plumber simply would not come. "Actually," she said, "there wasn't much to it. I got a book from the library, asked a lot of questions at the hardware store, and I did it."

Mallory shrugged off questions about his ranch. "Everything stays pretty much the same," he said. They had all been to his ranch apparently; no one pressed him.

When it was his turn, Lucas also shrugged; it was pitifully like a small boy trying to copy consciously an innate gesture of his older brother. "I'm the black sheep," he said. "I'm willing to let my wife support me."

I found myself growing hot and wanted to protest that it wasn't like that, but Mallory stood up then, finishing off his drink. "Let's take your stuff upstairs," he said. "Same old room. Maybe you'd like to stretch your legs after you get your bags up? Give Ginny time to rest a little before dinner. Still at seven, like always."

He wants to talk to Lucas obviously, and there must be many things to talk about. No one said anything about their father, how he is, if Lucas is expected to go to visit him, if I am.

The house is luxurious by any standard: so well built that no sound carries from one room to another, a private bath with each bedroom, and each room must have a magnificent view. From our windows I can see the sheep on the grassy hills: They could be pale rocks catching fire from the setting sun, turning red-gold all at once. I imagine Lucas spending hours at this window, looking at sheep on the hillside. He never mentioned it.

Was Mallory warning me that they dress for dinner? I thought of that suddenly with alarm. I had no formal clothes, only a long skirt and shirt that I sometimes wear at

home. I looked at them and reluctantly put them on. I was
feeling nervous, alone in a house where I didn't know the
rules, where everyone else communicated by oblique looks
and silences, where mention of the event that had brought
us all together was carefully avoided.

I wandered to the window again and looked out through
the deepening twilight. It seemed to bring the hills closer;
the sheep were like moonflowers growing in clumps here
and there. Mallory said it went on as far as you can see.
How big was it? Thousands of acres. It looked very expen-
sive, like the bluegrass country of Kentucky or the rolling
hills of Delaware and Virginia. The figure four thousand
an acre popped into my head as I watched the sheep vanish
into the darkening shadows. Why that figure? I kept saying
it to myself: four thousand an acre. Five thousand acres?
Six thousand? As far as you can see. The land is worth
millions. Lucas is in line to inherit a fortune. I can say it,
but it is an abstract; I can't believe it.

I wrote in this old notebook until I became too restless
to stay in the room waiting for Lucas to come home. I
looked out into the hallway and saw no one; there was no
sound. At the end of the corridor was a closed door; I
turned toward it, confused suddenly about how we had
come to our room. Up a rather narrow staircase, but at
which end of the hall? I went to the end door and stopped
with my hand on the knob. I looked back; all the doors
were closed. The hallway was paneled in a golden wood,
there was gold carpeting. There were lights in gold sconces
on the wall, and here and there between the doors there
were paintings that looked very good, oils, landscapes and
seascapes.

The doors should be numbered, or something, I thought
in dismay. I was no longer certain which one was my room;
with the realization, I turned the knob and pushed the end
door open enough to see through the crack. It was the
greenhouse balcony. Almost gaily I went into the plant
room.

The western sky was streaked with bands of midnight-
blue against violet; as I stood there several fluorescent lights
came on automatically, and the room was as bright as
midday. From below in the living room, the balcony had
seemed reasonably small, but from inside, there was no
way to estimate its size. The plants were everywhere, ob-
scuring walls and corners, giving the room the illusion of

stretching out into vast regions beyond the house. The effect was magical almost; even the ceiling was deceptively camouflaged by plants and slanting glass walls. It was possible to stand in the room and look at the sky overhead and imagine that a forest started on one side and cut the sky from view, and that there was a clearing to the west, ending in a sunset that was turning the horizon into a purple-violet band.

The plants all looked healthy and lush, and the air smelled good among them: damp earth mixed with sunshine, I thought in surprise. I never had considered what good earth actually smelled like. I touched a waxy leaf, smelled a blossom or two, and wandered closer to the south window wall; I could see the pond in the distance, and two dark figures walking slowly. Mallory and Lucas were coming back. As I watched them, the thought came to mè that one of the Culbertson children, probably Mallory, would inherit the land. Was that why he had been summoned? To break the news that the land was indivisible, that one of them would inherit it all? I shook my head at the idea. Insane. Of course the estate would be sold and the proceeds distributed among the children.

Mallory and Lucas disappeared among the dogwood trees that had become lumpish shadows, and with them gone I suddenly felt exposed standing before the window wall. I was a trespasser in this room, in this house. I backed away from the window between benches of African violets and brilliant gloxinias. The shadows of the trees seemed to swell, to press against the glass, hiding the world beyond, and a sensation of vertigo overcame me as the fluorescent lights went out. The living room lights went out. I reached for something to catch my balance and in the moment that I groped for the nearest bench I had the impression that the room was bare, there were no tables, no plants, no musty earth smells. Instead there was sawdust and raw wood. The room was unfinished and I was not alone. I took another step backward, looking right and left, searching for whoever was there with me. I could see no one in the darkness, but he was near, coming nearer.

I backed away another step and a new surge of vertigo swept over me. There was no railing, nothing to stop me; I felt myself falling as he reached out, and now I could smell alcohol and cologne and wet wool. Desperately I swung around and grasped for something to hold on to, something to stop my fall.

I was on my knees at the head of the curved staircase, holding on to the railing with both hands, blinking in the bright light. Once more the air was pungent with growing plants and soil; the lights were on as before and there was the lingering sunset beyond the glass wall.

I shook my head and started down, holding tightly to the banister all the way. I was muttering to myself, something about drinks before dinner on an empty stomach, and fatigue, but at the bottom, I looked up one more time, and I knew I would not go up there again.

There were two newcomers at dinner, Dr. Sizemore and Professor Hugh Froelich. Dr. Sizemore said How do you do, and then not another word. He is sixty at least, a gray man who picked at his food absently and looked at his watch a lot. Professor Froelich is in his thirties; he looks like an athlete: compact, muscular, and alert, a sprinter waiting for the starting whistle all the time. His tension is tiresome. Also at dinner I met Anita Mantessa who cooks and does the housework. She is a tall handsome woman with jet-black hair and ivory skin; her cooking is of master-chef quality. Dinner was buffet style. If you want anything, please ring, she said softly and vanished, into the kitchen presumably. The food was in casserole and chafing dishes; the salad on a bed of ice.

"Without chemistry we'd all be dead," Conrad was saying to Janet, evidently picking up an old argument.

"Quicker than we'd be dead with it? He spends his time looking for better ways to kill plants," Janet said to me.

"Herbicides," Conrad said tonelessly, the way he had told her to shut up earlier, in a dead voice that revealed nothing.

Dr. Sizemore looked at his watch and pushed a piece of roast beef around on his plate. He looked at his watch again. The lights flickered several times during dinner, and that reassured me; more than likely they went out often here in the country. A brief outage had caught me in the plant room. Hugh Froelich was explaining the electroen-cephalograph to Mallory, who looked bored and tired. Lucas felt my thigh under the table, gave it a gentle squeeze, as if to say, Buck up, we won't be here very long. I put my hand on his and for a moment we held hands under the table. As I caught Mallory's glance I felt my cheeks grow hot; he smiled at me in a kind, very wise way. Married two years, I thought, and people still looked at us with that sympathetic and knowing expression. I pretended to be interested in Janet's diatribe against chemicals. Conrad was deliberately ignoring her; she was furious and red-faced, hissing at him about poisons and selling out.

"Ah, Janet . . . ah, everyone," Dr. Sizemore said then, standing up. "It is eight-thirty, and I promised your father that he could visit with you for just a few minutes at this time."

The silence was prolonged and intense; no one moved.

Dr. Sizemore looked unhappy with his chore and with the assembled members of the family. "He's dying," he said, "but you all know that. I beg of you, no shouting, no excitement, no arguments . . ."

I found myself staring at them one after another. What kind of people were they that the doctor had to tell them not to yell at their dying father? None of them met my gaze; they didn't see me at all. I reached for Lucas's hand again, but he was unresponsive; not cold, simply absent.

Dr. Sizemore took a deep breath. "Let's get it over with," he said and led the way from the room, through the wide hallway toward the back of the house. We turned down a narrower passage that followed the curved wall of the stairs, toward a room under the balcony, part of the new addition to the house. Dr. Sizemore said, "We moved him to the sunroom some time ago. It's easy to get him outside to the garden from here. He likes that." He cleared his throat nervously and pushed open a door at the end of the hallway. We all followed him.

Most of the room was in shadow. The south wall was closed off by drapes, and there were hanging baskets of plants from the inner edge of the drapes to about four feet inside the room: fuchsias, begonias, geraniums, spider plants, trailing orchids, plants I had never seen before. The furniture was wicker, with soft-colored cushions and covers; there was a hospital bed with two nightstands. A woman was standing by the bed.

I hung back as the others moved together closer to the bed. I had not realized how very old he was; Lucas had told me he was in his eighties, but he looked more like a hundred, or two hundred: shriveled and brown, as if he had already started to mummify. Only his eyes were alive as they sought out each face in turn. His eyes seemed to be looking out through a layer of gauze. I felt a chill when his gaze found me and held, then moved on.

I forced myself to stop looking at him and examined the woman instead. Greta? I had expected something else: a beautiful woman? a fortune hunter? what? I couldn't say. She was plain, pleasant looking, intelligent looking. She could have been a nurse, I thought, and it occurred to me that perhaps she was the nurse, not Greta at all. But when I saw how her hand rested on his shoulder, I knew this was the fourth and last wife. She was fair, sturdily built, in her early forties and not trying to pretend she wasn't. At the far side of the room someone stirred, and another figure took shape as a man moved into the lighted area of the bed.

"Bill Strohm," Mallory said without surprise. "You know Conrad. This is Lucas and his wife, Ginny. You remember Janet, of course."

"Of course," Strohm said. "Ladies and gentlemen, this is a difficult evening for all of you, I'm sure. I have been ordered to play a tape for you at this time, and for that reason I have arranged those chairs in a comfortable way, I trust. If you will be seated. Dr. Sizemore, you've given your patient permission to participate in this event?"

"Ah, yes," Dr. Sizemore said miserably, denying the words even as he uttered them. His permission, I thought disdainfully. That old man had ordered him, just as he had ordered Strohm, just as he must order everyone who came into contact with him. At least Strohm was honest about it.

As soon as we were seated in a circle around a glass-topped table, Bill Strohm again took charge. "I have here an affidavit attesting to the authenticity of the tape you will hear shortly. I have copies of the affidavit for each of you. The tape was made last March."

In the dim light it was easy to forget about Janet's gross body; her face was lovely, shadowed, her eyes luminous. Conrad's face was invisible; I could see only his silhouette against the background light. On the other side of Janet was Mallory, hard and tight looking. Lucas came next, and I, and then Bill Strohm. A seance, I thought with alarm. It was just like a seance, except that the body was still warm, very much present, and in command.

In the center of the table was the tape recorder, a large professional-looking model. Bill Strohm flicked a switch, adjusted a dial, and sat back. There was a moment of whirring sound, followed by a thin, dry voice, like wind through loose sand.

"I have asked you to come in order to explain the conditions of my will. I know the matter is of the utmost interest to each of you." There was another moment of the background whirring; he continued by introducing Bill Strohm, his attorney. Strohm spoke briefly, identifying himself, giving the date and time of day. Dr. Sizemore was there; he spoke even more briefly, saying only that John Daniel Culbertson was of sound mind and in full possession of his faculties. I looked at Professor Hugh Froelich in surprise when his name was mentioned. He had been present also. Now he was standing apart from the group at the table, watching closely.

Mr. Culbertson talked then about his investments; he planned to liquidate them during the coming months, he said, and while the resulting cash would be a sizeable sum, it was, of course, the land itself that would make up the bulk of his estate. He began to cough, and yelled hoarsely, "Turn that goddam thing—"

More background noise, then he resumed. "One of you will inherit the farm, all of it in a piece. Which one will be determined by me, following a period of one week from the day of my burial. During that period each of you will remain here in my house. You will bring in no outsiders, nor will you spend a night away from the house. These are the people who will live here during this one-week period: Mallory, Conrad, Janet, Lucas, and his wife, if he wishes her to stay. Professor Hugh Froelich will be permitted to remain. Anita Mantessa will take care of the house and Carlos will manage the farm, as each has done for the past few years. No one else is permitted to live in the house during your period of bereavement."

I was looking at him on the bed; it had been raised to an almost sitting position. He was watching us intently, listening to the tape along with everyone else. He looked like a death's head. He focused on me, and I felt impaled. I jerked my whole body around to break free of his gaze.

"During this last visit, each of you will cooperate with Professor Froelich in order that he may record your electroencephalograms. One week from the day of my funeral, whenever it occurs, you will allow him to make a new EEG. The following day you will assemble here for the

reading of my will. There is a certain test I've prepared for
you that will be given on that day. No one, not even Bill
Strohm, knows what it is. If one of you passes it, that one
will be the legal heir to the real estate. You will share
equally in the proceeds from the sale of my other assets.
My wife, Greta, has already been provided for to our
mutual satisfaction. It is agreed that the day following my
death, she will depart and make no further claims on my
estate."

Mallory jumped to his feet. He broke the circle, I
thought wildly, terrified that something awful would happen.

"This is crazy!" Mallory cried. "I'm going home!"

"Sit down!" It was a whisper from the bed; the thin, dry
voice had failed even more and was hardly audible.

"Mallory," Bill Strohm said, "please sit down and let's
finish this. I assure you, it's all legal. You are free to leave,
of course, but if you don't agree to follow instructions,
comply with your father's wishes, you automatically exclude
yourself from any future consideration in the inheritance
of the land holdings."

Lucas caught Mallory's arm and pulled him back to his
chair. "Take it easy," he said. "Let's hear it out."

There was very little more on the tape. There were instructions to the heirs to cooperate with Bill Strohm and
follow his orders to the letter.

Or be excommunicated, I thought.

The whirring sound came back, and this time it was
followed by Bill Strohm's voice repeating the details of the
taping, adding the exact length of the tape we had just
heard. He turned the machine off.

"Now get out!" whispered the dying man on the hospital
bed. He closed his eyes and for a moment I thought he had
died right then. Dr. Sizemore was on one side, Greta on
the other, as if to protect him from his children.

Mallory stood up so abruptly he overturned his chair.
He didn't stop, but left the room without a word. Janet
went to the foot of the bed and stared at the old man; her
back was to me. She followed Mallory. Conrad was at her
side by the time they got to the door. Lucas had not moved
yet. I started to walk to the door, expecting him to join
me, but he continued to sit before the glass-topped table,
staring at the tape recorder. I hesitated, and left alone.
When I reached the living room, only Mallory was there.

"They went out for some fresh air, or something," he said vaguely. "Sorry you walked into such a mess, Ginny. Tomorrow we'll all go home and forget this. Okay?"

I nodded, not believing any of it, not what I had just seen in the old man's room, not what I was hearing then.

"Why?" I asked, hardly even knowing what the question meant, how much I was asking him to explain.

For a moment Mallory looked at me with an expression that reminded me of the look on my father's face the day I told him I planned to get married. Hurt, vulnerable, aching in a mysterious way, that was what his look had made me think, that was what Mallory's look made me think. He turned away without speaking, and from the doorway it was Lucas who answered.

"He hates us because he knows we know he's a wife killer," he said. "All my life he's been punishing me for knowing what he is. He wants to keep on after he dies, forever. And that goddamn psychologist is helping him!" Lucas looked pale and sick, the way he had looked when his fever broke when he had the flu. He sounded drunk. He was not looking at Mallory or me, but was watching the hallway. "Actually, he killed all his wives, until this one, didn't he, Mallory?" Lucas glanced at his brother with a bitter expression. "Tell her about Janet's mother."

Mallory shrugged. "You'll hear it sooner or later. Might as well be from one of the principals. Conrad and I heard the fight he had with Janet's mother the night she died. They were at the top of the stairs to the balcony." He nodded at the curved staircase, then turned his back on it. "We heard them. This part of the house wasn't finished yet. We weren't supposed to be in here. No one knew we had sneaked in. When she fell, she never uttered a sound. He had broken her neck before she went over."

I stared at him, afraid to look at the stairs, the balcony where I had smelled sawdust and new, raw wood. I could feel goosebumps on my arms and legs. "Didn't you tell anyone?" I asked; my voice came out in a whisper.

"I told," he said. "No one believed me. He proved he wasn't even home that night."

I forced myself to look at Lucas by the hallway door, paying little attention to Mallory and me. He was listening, I thought, waiting for someone, the doctor, the lawyer, or Froelich.

"Lucas will have to tell you about his mother," Mallory

said. "We had all left by then, except him." He went to the bar and poured himself a glass of bourbon. He didn't bother with the ice this time.

At that moment Hugh Froelich and Bill Strohm appeared in the doorway. Lucas leaped at Froelich and knocked him backward, fell to the floor with him. Strohm was too surprised to interfere for several seconds. By the time he reacted, Mallory was there pulling Lucas away.

"You crazy son of a bitch!" he yelled. "What the hell do you think you're doing?"

"Ask him what he's doing! What kind of game is this? What's he doing here with all that crap about EEGs? Let him go to a loony bin to play his fucking head games." Lucas was panting; his face was pale and shiny with sweat.

I had known from the first that Lucas hated and feared psychologists and psychiatrists with such unyielding vehemence that I had always avoided any conversation about either, or their work. He had told me early in our relationship that psychiatrists had tried to get him to admit black was white, that they had almost destroyed him when he refused. Sometime, I had promised myself, sometime when everything had been smooth and calm for a long while, when we were both working happily, when we were healthy and relaxed and had no financial worries, sometime in a future that was dim and distant, I would find out exactly what had happened to him, what the psychiatrists had done, or what he thought they had tried to do. Sometime. During the two years of our marriage that time had not arrived.

Sizemore came hurrying down the hall; he helped Froelich up. Automatically he looked at his eyes and felt his pulse.

"I'm okay," Froelich said irritably. "It's okay. I don't blame him. Forget it. I want a drink." He pulled free of Sizemore and headed for the liquor.

"Is there coffee?" Strohm asked. He saw it on another table and helped himself. "Mallory, I want to talk to all of you for just a minute. Where's Janet and Conrad?"

"Right here," Conrad said. I hadn't seen them enter and had no idea how long they had been back. Janet looked very frightened, Conrad bored and sleepy.

"Right. This isn't going to take long. Last winter your father had a heart attack, right? He thought he was dying and he was mad as hell. He can't stand the idea of leaving the farm to any of you. He wants it to go when he goes I guess. Anyway, he already had a will, a perfectly ordinary will dividing everything among all of you, the farm incorporated. No favorites. He called me over; he wanted a new will, he said. Okay, I'm a lawyer and he's a client. Period. I can advise him, but I can't make him do anything he doesn't want to do. I did advise him. Until I was blue in the face. And we ended up with this goddam foolishness. He had me research what he wanted done, to make sure it was legal and would hold up if any of you contests it. It'll hold up. I wish to God I had been able to find a loophole. It's his land. He can dictate the conditions of his will. So we play his game for seven days following the funeral. I just want to warn you that when he dies you'd better get back here. If you don't play it his way, you're out. You'll get your share of the cash and not a cent more."

"What's the test he's rigged up for us?" Conrad asked.

"I don't know. In the office safe, we have his original will and a sealed envelope. There are copies of both in his safe here. I haven't got a clue about what's in the sealed envelope."

"If one of us passes the test, that one inherits all the land, the house, barns, livestock, everything?" Mallory asked. Bill Strohm nodded and started to speak, but Mallory was not done yet. "What's to prevent that one from selling and splitting everything with the others?"

"Nothing," Bill Strohm said bitterly. "That's why this is absolute rot. As soon as one of you is named the beneficiary, the game ends. What you do with it after that is up to you."

"And what if none of us passes? What happens to the land then?"

Bill Strohm's mouth tightened into a grim line before he answered. "The land will go to Oregon State University, to be used as an experimental farm."

I gasped before I could stop myself. No one moved or said anything until Conrad began to laugh. Janet glared at him.

"Don't you see?" Conrad said softly. "It's always been us against him. And now he's going to make it us against us. What he never could do in life, he's going to try to do after death."

"It won't work," Mallory said, looking at the others one by one. "I say right now that if I'm the one, I'll sell it just as fast as I can find a buyer. It will be split four ways. I swear it."

"Me too," Lucas said quickly.

Janet nodded, moistened her lips, then murmured. "And I."

"It's easy enough to say it now, but what will the winner say later?" Conrad asked thoughtfully. "I'll go along, of course. God knows I wouldn't want the farm."

"I'm off," Bill Strohm said, putting down his coffee cup. "Hell of an evening. Hell of a way to go."

He was really angry, I realized. He had been put in a humiliating position and it infuriated him. If there had been a way to forestall this, he would have found it if only to avoid both the scene he had just played out in the old man's room and the coming scenes that he obviously dreaded.

"Now you," Mallory said, turning to Professor Hugh Froelich. "What's your part in this?"

Sizemore had been leaning against the doorframe; he pulled away from it and said hurriedly, "I'll leave too. Greta will call me if there's any change. Good night, good night."

Hugh Froelich watched him and Strohm leave before he answered Mallory. "He has a lot of power," he said, indicating the back of the house. "He gets what he wants, obviously always has. A few years ago I wrote a paper that he read and became interested in. I was summoned to meet him. I was curious, and I came to dinner. He pumped me about my paper, and demanded a reading list, reference books, articles. And he called my department head to make sure I carried out his orders. I sent the stuff, and eventually it was returned and I put it all out of mind. Last spring he sent for me again."

He finished his drink, poured himself another. Lucas was watching Froelich the way a dog watches a snake, waiting for the instant when it is safe to grab it by the neck. I moved closer to Lucas, wishing he would become aware of me, wishing he would come back from wherever it was he had gone.

"This time," Froelich said, "he was different. He was sick, for one thing. It was soon after his heart attack and he looked like a dying man. But his mind was as lucid as ever, I guess. He was giving orders like a man who expects to be obeyed. He told me what I was to do, give you all the

EEGs now and again a week after his death. He gave me a copy of one that he had had made some years ago. It was his scheme from the start," he said, glancing at Lucas.

"I bet!" Lucas muttered.

"You're willing to go along with his madness for a price, I take it," Mallory said.

"The university administration knows they stand in line to inherit about twenty million dollars' worth of property," Froelich said. "How much choice do you think I have? If I don't do it, someone else will, and it is my baby, after all."

"What was in that paper?" Conrad asked then.

"I proposed a method to disprove once and for all that spirit possession can take place. It was at the height of that craze a few years ago. The electroencephalograph records brain activities, the various waves, as you know. Each tracing is unique, just like fingerprints, or the retinas of the eyes. And the waves change. Learning, for example, has a physiological effect on the brain; there are actual changes that can be demonstrated. Learning, growing, experiences, everything you do and think and study, everything that happens to you throughout your life is recorded in the brain. In my paper I suggested that if possession actually took place, the brain must be altered, must become like the brain of the possessor, or the behavior of the possessed wouldn't change." He stopped, then took a deep drink. "But you don't want a lecture tonight. My paper's in his library, along with quite a complete collection of works on possession. I'll go over it with any of you tomorrow if you like."

"Possession," Janet whispered. "He thinks he can possess one of us? Is that what he intends to try?"

"He is crazy!" Mallory said, almost jubilantly. "No court would allow this nonsense to determine the outcome of a multimillion-dollar legacy!"

Hugh Froelich shook his head. "You don't understand," he said. "He's doing this as a humanitarian gesture, knowing he's dying. He's participating in an experiment to prove that possession is impossible. The tracings will prove it. No change will show up in the EEGs."

I felt numb. I couldn't follow the reasoning, or understand the fury that crossed Conrad's face, or comprehend the tautness of Lucas beside me on the couch.

"Professor," Conrad said coolly, "you and I both know this is a crock of shit."

"Why?" Janet asked. "What does that mean?"

"You can't prove a theory with negative evidence," Hugh Froelich said. "I told him that. It's worthless data, if any data comes from it. He understands that exactly."

No one spoke for a long time, until Mallory broke the silence. His voice was thick, almost blurred, as if all at once the liquor had taken effect.

"For a week we sit here and watch each other for a sign, for a change, for anything to indicate that he's taking over, or trying to. We feel his presence worming in and out, relive every goddam nightmare. And then the test that no one will be able to pass. And finally the will, hearing it officially announced that this property is being donated to the university. Pretty, isn't it? An old man's last little joke on his kids. Laughing all the way to hell. Well, fuck him! I'm going home in the morning."

It broke up with that. Lucas dug his fingers into my arm so hard I cried out, and instantly regretted it. I thought he was going to weep, and I realized how extraordinarily tired we both were. It was midnight, but we were on East Coast time and had been up for almost twenty hours.

In our room Lucas paced, then sat on the side of the bed and held his head in both hands and finally said he had to walk.

Now I should write my own interpretations of this insane day, but my mind is too blank. I wish Lucas would come back and hold me until we both can fall asleep. I want to tell him how much I love him and how sorry I am. How very sorry I am for all this. I wish we had pushed the beds together before he went out.

October 15

I woke up first this morning. Although I tried to go back to sleep, it was impossible; finally I got up and dressed without waking Lucas. He was sleeping like a child, face in his pillow, the way he must have slept when he lived here. He looked young enough to be that schoolboy.

It was only seven, ten by my East Coast body rhythm; I expected no one else to be stirring yet and was surprised to find Mallory already having coffee when I went to the kitchen.

"I smelled the coffee," I said lamely.

"And good morning to you, too," he said. "Luke still sacked out?" He got a second mug from a cabinet and poured coffee for me. "Cream and sugar in the breakfast room. You want anything else yet?"

"No thanks. He's sound asleep."

"Yeah. He was pretty tired when he finally left me last night."

We went into the adjoining room where sunlight fired scarlet geraniums. This was the brightest room I had seen yet in this house, blue and yellow wallpaper, yellow furniture, white woodwork. "I've never seen so many plants in one house before."

"He likes them." Mallory sat down with his back to the windows. There were no curtains; there was a picture-postcard mountain scene instead. Apparently every window overlooked a breathtaking vista. "What do you do?" Mallory asked.

"I'm an editorial assistant. I read manuscripts and report

on them, write routine letters, things like that. You have a ranch in Oregon?"

"Eastern Oregon, high prairie country, not like this valley. Thousand acres of wheat, thousand of grazing land. Bone-dry most of the time, rocky all the time, bitter cold in the winter and hot as hell in the summer. Not like the valley."

I could read nothing into his voice, or the words. I could not tell if he loved or hated the lush valley, if he loved or hated his ranch. We had flown over eastern Oregon and I had thought it a wasteland, nothing but desert. I drank my coffee.

"Sit still," he said. "I'll bring the pot back." He left and a moment later brought in the coffeepot and refilled both cups. "What's wrong with Luke?" he asked, looking at me intently.

"Nothing. Why?"

"He's changed."

"He's just getting over the flu. I guess he's thinner than he was before he got sick."

"You kids eating enough?"

My cheeks burned; I ducked my head and looked at the coffee mug. "We get by."

"Yeah. He told me he's a set designer. Is he successful?"

"He's awfully good," I said with a touch of sharpness.

He did not press the issue, as if I had answered his question. I supposed I had and that made me angrier.

"Why the inquisition?" I demanded. "He hasn't asked you for money or anything. He'd rather die on the spot than ask you for money."

"Ginny, has Luke told you anything about me? How I've always felt about him?"

I nodded.

"Okay. Can you two get by without the money? If you knew there was no way on earth you could ever touch a cent of it, would it bother you?"

"I didn't even know there might be money," I said, swallowing the first reply that formed. He wasn't prying or picking on me. There was a crease between his eyes; he was leaning forward watching me, waiting. He was deeply worried. His concern was not for me; it was for Lucas. The warmth I had felt for him before flooded back in, driving out my anger. "We would get by exactly as we have in the past. We don't have much money, as you seem to know already. Lucas doesn't make much yet. He's had three jobs in the past two years. He is very good, but it's a rough business and it will take a long time for him to get established. I don't make very much either. But it's enough."

He began to tap his fingers and now he was looking past me, scowling. "There's going to be ten, fifteen thousand for each of us outright. Maybe twice that. Tell him to take it and run, Ginny. Can you persuade him to do that, do you think?"

I stared at him. "Why? Why would it be so bad for all of you to live in this house for a week? It would take that long just to do an inventory, to make decisions about things, like that clock, for instance. What happens to something like the clock?"

The clock I pointed to was a blue Delft antique on a wall where a dozen beautiful plates were mounted. "You'll have to have appraisals on everything in the house. That clock must be worth hundreds of dollars."

"Everything stays, remember? Winner gets all."

"But you agreed that the winner is going to sell it all and divide the proceeds."

"There won't be a winner," he said tiredly, "except the university. Luke doesn't believe that, and I guess Conrad and Janet agree with him, but there won't be a winner. It's a charade, a game. What'll happen when Luke sweats out that damn week and dreams of all that money, and then finds out that there isn't any winner? Can he take that?"

I didn't know. I thought of the various grandiose schemes Lucas had talked about from time to time: travel, a house in the country with an orchard and open fields, an apartment in the city . . . Neither of us had believed for a minute that it was a possibility or could ever become a possibility. One of us hadn't believed, I thought suddenly. I had thought it nothing more than a game. I was not even good at playing such a game; my list of wants and wishes always stopped at a bigger apartment and more clothes and a savings account for emergencies. Would it be possible to persuade him to stop at fifty thousand even, when there were millions within reach? Maybe, I decided; if we were back home and he was working at a job that he was excited about, and if we had no pressing bills at the moment.

I watched Mallory without trying to answer his question. He knew, probably better than I, if Lucas would be able to handle it if the prize was snatched away at the last minute. Too many ifs, I thought. It was raining ifs.

"Try, Ginny," he said softly. "When *he* dies, don't let Luke come back. Today we're all going down to make that goddam EEG, and afterward you and Luke will take off. He promised not to stay any longer than that. When you get home, try to make him give up the idea of playing games with the old man. It's a no-win game every time. Luke knows that, we all know it. Make him realize he knows it. I'm going to get my own lawyer to work, try to break that will, but Bill may be right in saying it's fool-proof."

"Why are you agreeing to the EEG?"

"Because I told Luke I would if he would promise to get the hell out of here this evening." He looked naked, helpless; it was clear that the love he felt for Lucas had not diminished over the years. He must have seen something of my understanding then, for he got up abruptly and left, saying he liked a walk before breakfast.

They all went out before ten o'clock. Lucas and I haven't had any time together since we got here. Even though I knew I was as restless and fretful as a child, I couldn't help feeling resentful, excluded from an intimate circle where the initiates could speak in half sentences or single words, or even with significant looks, and be thoroughly understood by the others. I, the outsider, understood nothing.

I explored the house, skirted the shelves of books on occultism in the library, ignored the hanging garden, and, of course, the back half of the house where he was dying.

After I packed the few things we had unpacked, I sat looking at the sheep on the hills. My restlessness drove me out for a walk. The day was warm and the air dry, the sky cloudless. Not at all my idea of Oregon, I thought. The gardens were as lovely as any I had ever seen. Everything was trimmed and neatly mulched with bark; the roses were in beds with bark paths winding in and out among them. I studied the rose beds: There was something . . . I realized how carefully the roses had been laid out, not only for size and variety, but for color. White, immaculate, pristine, gave way to ivory, and on into the yellows; pinks, so pale the tint looked illusory, blended into deeper pinks, reds, nearly black. Corals, oranges, a group that was almost mahogany. I looked back at the house; from there, from any distance at all, the colors would look like an impressionist painting. There were chrysanthemums and staked dahlias, some of the flowers as big as platters. I was too close to see the effect of the color arrangement. They were meant to be seen close up as individual blooms and from farther away as larger patterns of light and color. I scanned the house —up there, I thought, those windows. I didn't know whose windows they were. *His* I suspected. I wandered along the walks until I came to a shadowy moist area where ferns grew as high as my head, and vines crawled up posts, clung to an overhead latticework of wood. Hanging baskets of fuchsias dominated here.

Suddenly I felt it again, the same certainty that I had felt in the hanging garden. Someone was near, watching me. I stopped. Something was telling me to get out, get out, get out. I wanted to run, but I was too frightened to move. It vanished as quickly as it started, and a wave of nausea passed over me. I turned around and found myself looking at the sunroom, through the glass, where he was lying in bed, staring at me.

"You're dead," I heard my own voice say. "You're dead!"

Greta ran across the room to his side. She felt his pulse, reached into the drawer of the table by the bed, withdrew a stethoscope and used it. I watched her close his eyes and pull the sheet over his face, watched her go to a chair by an end table, sit down, and dial the telephone.

I didn't know I had been moving until I realized I was on the lawn in the hot sunshine. I was shaking violently; nausea came over me in surges, each one stronger, until I retched and heaved convulsively, clinging to a tree trunk.

Now I'm in our room, staring out the window again. The sheep are still there. Don't they ever move? All I can think of is turning around to see him watching me. Seeing him dead, dying. Dead. We won't leave now. I know it as surely as I know that the game has started and he has won the first round.

When I could no longer stand our room, I went downstairs to the library to try to find something to read, but I kept looking at the books on possession, until finally I felt driven outside again. This time I headed for the red lava road that went toward the hills. I walked for an hour and when I came back I saw the station wagon in the drive.

Hugh Froelich met me at the door. "We were worried about you," he said. "You know?"

I nodded. "Where's Lucas?"

"In the library with the others. Bill Strohm is with them. They've already taken the . . . Mr. Culbertson away to the funeral home."

We sat in the living room waiting for the others to finish their meeting. Neither of us talked. Hugh Froelich was still wound up tight, I thought. If he was like this all the time, he would have a heart attack or a stroke. The house was very quiet, until someone opened the library door, and I could hear Mallory yelling. A moment later he appeared in the doorway, nodded to us, left again. His face was red, furious.

I hurried to the library and met Lucas in the hall. "Let's go upstairs," he said in a hard voice.

"Mallory called his lawyer," he said in our room. "Strohm talked to him, and they agreed that we have to go through with the terms of the will or lose out immediately. They don't like it, but we're stuck with it. Mallory's madder than hell. He's staying, though."

I stood by the door as he swung back and forth across the room. He looked ready to kick something or throw something. His hands clenched, relaxed, clenched again, and his cheek twitched. With his back to me, he said, "You're getting the hell out of here tonight. I'll take you to the airport."

"No. I'll call in tomorrow and tell them I won't be back for a week or so. I don't want to leave you now."

"We don't want you here," he said, still facing away, standing rigidly at the window.

I went to him, touched his arm. It felt like wood. "Lucas, what else is it? Something else has happened, hasn't it? What?"

"You have to go. That's all."

I stepped around to look at his face. He was so pale I was afraid he might faint. "What else?"

He grabbed me with an intensity that was frightening. He held me hard against him, his cheek on my head. "God, I love you," he said hoarsely. "You can't stay. I'm afraid. Please, just go." He talked into my hair, most of it inaudible, and then he was weeping.

I got him to the bed and sat holding him while great sobs tore through him. When it was over I went for a washcloth and a glass of water for him. He lay on his back with one arm over his face.

"Are you all right?" I asked, wiping his forehead with the cloth. He took it from me and ran it over his face.

"It's okay," he said. "We all agreed that you should leave," he went on. "He told Greta that you had to have an EEG made too. She said he was raving about you, at times thinking you were Sally or Viola, one of his wives. She said he went on about you during the night and again this morning."

I watched my hand holding the water glass; when the shaking got so hard that water was sloshing over the rim, I put the glass down on the bedside table. "I don't believe in any of that," I said, relieved that my voice was normal. "And you don't either. None of you believes in it. It's crazy for anyone to get upset over something no one believes in."

Lucas made no response for a long time. Then he sat up. He picked up the glass and drank the water, finishing it all. "I know," he said. "It's crazy. He was crazy. We all look like our mothers, but inside, he's there, in each one of us. It's going to be a hellish week, Regina. We may end up killing each other. He knew that when he made his will over. That's why he did it. That's what I mean by crazy. Crazy mean. Crazy hateful. I don't want you here this coming week. It'll be easier if you aren't here."

I shook my head. "I won't make an EEG. I won't play. But I won't leave you here. Both of us, however it is, both leave or both stay."

He put down the glass and reached for me. His arms were gentle now, and his kiss, and when we made love, it was sweet and gentle. Afterward we lay in each other's arms for a long time not moving, not talking, content with the closeness.

Lying with his arms around me, I realized I could not tell him what had happened that day outside his father's windows or yesterday in the plant room. I would think about it later, try to fathom the reason for not confiding in him for the first time since we met. We were already changing, we already had lost something. Maybe one day when we were both old, when this was all a very distant past, we would find that something again; maybe then I would talk about it.

I must have drowsed; he woke me by getting up to go

to the bathroom. The shower came on and presently he returned with a towel around his waist. He sat on the side of the bed and stroked my hair.

"It's going to be hardest for Janet and Conrad," he said, tracing my eyebrow, running his finger along my nose. "Your freckles are all gone. I miss them."

"Idiot. I'll grow more. Why Janet and Conrad?"

"They had a thing for a while," he said. "When they were just kids. She was really pretty, like a little movie star, and he was handsome and tall. Mallory had gone by then, and I was too young for them to bother with very much. Anyway, *he* caught them kissing or something. I'm almost certain it never got beyond that, but maybe it did. She was twelve, Conrad was seventeen. *He* almost killed Janet. My mother separated them, and he knocked her around some. She wrapped us both up and ran away for a couple of months. We went down to San Francisco."

"Why did she come back?"

"I never knew. I was only five or six. But everything changed after that. Conrad joined the army, and Janet was different, scared and moody. When she was sixteen, she left and I doubt that she ever came back until now. She went to one school after another, flunked out or ran away or something, over and over. Conrad never came back and Mallory only a couple of times, both of them for my sake." He was looking beyond me at the windows. Seeing the past? Seeing Janet as she had been? I felt certain he was not seeing the hills dotted with sheep.

"What happened with your mother?"

"They fought a lot after we came back home. I don't remember if they had very much before that. That last day they were fighting. I don't know about what. Sometimes it was her spending or his rages at one of the hired hands; sometimes over me, over something I had done. He never touched me. I think she must have told him that if he ever did, she would take me away for good. That day I was in the plant room reading. I used to like it up there. I heard a car roar out of the driveway and I saw her driving up the road and saw the truck cutting across the field, right through the fence. I watched it all from the plant room windows. He beat her to the bridge and when she got there, he pulled out just in front of her and she swerved and hit the abutment. Her car turned over and rolled down into the river. He backed up the truck into the field a little

bit so that only his front wheels were on the shoulder of
the road. By then other people were running from the barn,
and it looked as if he had just stopped and was getting out
to try to help her or something. That's what they all said.
That's what he said."

"What did you do?" I asked in a whisper. I was shivering. His voice was flat and dead; it was as if they had all
learned from a common source how to hide behind a
monotone.

Lucas got up and walked to the window. With his back
to me, he said, "I went crazy. I ran away, and when they
found me, I told them Mallory was my father. The state
police took me to him. I couldn't remember anything about
it. In my senior year at Columbia I cracked up and had
therapy. Gradually I did remember. The counselor, and
later a shrink, both tried to make me admit I was mistaken.
They wanted to make it all neat and tidy, a Freudian nightmare. They wanted me to admit that I blamed him for her
death because I was jealous, all that crap. I thought I'd
really go crazy and finally I walked out on the lot of them
and came back to ask Mallory what I should do. He said
nothing. There was nothing I could do. I realized that he
had known from the start, or had suspected. He had prayed
that I'd never remember. He was good to me. If he hadn't
been there . . . I don't know what would have happened.
Anyway, I was able to live with it as long as I stayed the
hell away from here, away from him, and I did that."

I went to him and put my arms around him, but he was
rigid and distant. "Lucas, you couldn't help any of that.
You were a small child. It was self-protection that made
you forget. Even if you hadn't forgotten, there was nothing you could have done."

"You have to know it all," he said distantly and coldly.
"See why we don't want you here now? There's so much
ugliness here, we're all part of it. We're all so full of hate,
we're twisted inside. I thought his death would end it, instead there's just a new beginning. Mallory's right about
the land. It'll go to the university, yet none of us can leave
until it's over. He's still giving orders and we're saluting.
But not you, Regina. Not you."

I put my fingers on his lips. "It's you and me, kid," I
said. "Remember? You and me all the way."

He came back then and held me. "Nothing's going to
happen," he said fiercely. "We might all have a few night-

mares to get out of our systems, but that's all. Nothing else is going to happen."

The funeral will be tomorrow, October 16. Wednesday the funeral director will scatter his ashes over the farm. There won't be a ceremony. None of us will even be there. And on the twenty-fourth we'll go home. This will all be over. Eight days isn't very long.

October 16

I SHOULD HAVE brought some work with me, but, of course, I didn't expect to stay more than a day or two. Lucas, Mallory, and Conrad are playing poker. Janet is working on needlepoint, a piece as big as a door, filled with intricate flowers and medieval figures. Probably there is a unicorn, it's that kind of hanging. Janet is dieting. She must have told Anita Mantessa, but she hasn't mentioned it in my hearing. She turned down offers of a drink, took no dessert, no second helpings of anything, and seemed to eat only fruit all day. Conrad has started to smoke after giving it up for nearly ten years. He chain smokes.

"Funny," he said looking at his newly lighted cigarette right after dinner. "For years I never even thought of smoking; it wasn't hard to quit, nothing to it. I just stopped one day. And now I just started again. Must be the inaction. I haven't had time on my hands since . . . I don't even know when."

"I'm going to start going over the books tomorrow," Mallory said. "We're none of us used to not doing things. We should all try to keep busy."

Conrad laughed, but it was not malicious. He seemed genuinely amused, genuinely fond of his brother. "You haven't changed a bit over the years. Keep busy. Don't brood. Work until you're tired enough to fall asleep the instant you hit the bed."

"It all works," Mallory said a bit stiffly.

They started to play cards soon after that, and I read for a while; there was a complete collection of Sherlock

Holmes in the library, including some works I'd never seen. I found my mind wandering and I picked up the notebook again. How good it must be, I thought, to know you have a family that cares for you, brothers who care, a sister who cares. I, an only child, could almost envy them the easy companionship they displayed for each other, the automatic concern they showed, the understanding. On this emotionally wearing day, the day of their father's funeral, they seemed especially loving with each other, and it was hard to remember that his legacy had been one of hatred. They don't talk about him—as if by not speaking they can deny his reality. I wonder if it wouldn't be better to talk about it, the will, him, everything.

They will have to eventually, I know. The silence of avoidance is too hard to maintain. Apparently they were all terrorized and brutalized by their father; they all know terrible things about him. It will be ugly when it breaks out into the open, but it will have the ugliness of a particularly damaging storm, and afterward there will be the same freshness in the air, the same sense of renewal and re- growth.

I wrote those words and then stared at them and I could not comprehend why I had written them or what they meant. Platitudes, I thought. Mallory and his damn plati- tudes, me and mine.

Every time I looked up from the notebook, I found Hugh Froelich watching us, one after another. Not me, I wanted to tell him; I'm not part of this. But he watched me too.

No one wants to use the living room. After dinner Mal- lory led the way to the television room and everyone else followed as if it had been prearranged. This was the origi- nal living room, before the addition was built. It's large, very comfortable, with leather-covered furniture, an immense television, a pool table, game table, another fireplace. To- night we have a fire. They say the weather is due to change. It was brilliantly sunny again all day, no wind, no touch of autumn.

Today we all went to the funeral. No one else came. Anita Mantessa was told to turn away anyone who called.

My fingers are almost too stiff to write. And I have a headache. I noticed Janet glancing at the hall door again and again, and I found myself listening, trying to hear whatever it was that she evidently heard. There was nothing, but I'm sure that's what gave me the headache, the strain of trying to hear. I'm going to bed. Later I'll fill in details. I think the wind is starting to blow. One of the fir trees is rubbing against the house, it sounds like a whisper that is almost comprehensible.

October 17

I FELL ASLEEP almost as soon as I got to bed, and didn't hear Lucas when he came up. Later I woke up all at once, as if it were morning. The wind was blowing hard, rustling the drapes the way a woman rustles a long skirt as she walks. At first I thought it *was* a woman in a long skirt. I got up to close the window and looked out for a few minutes. The sky was light enough to see masses of clouds rolling in from the west, enclosing the moon, releasing it again. I wondered where the sheep were, if they were huddled together under the rising wind, too dumb to know a rain was coming, but uneasy.

That was me, I thought then. Uneasy. I looked at the bed, a lighter shadow among other shadows in the room, and I felt once more that it should be morning; I was ready to get up, dress, go down and face the day. The seventeenth, I thought with some satisfaction. One day down, seven to go. I wished again I had brought some work with me. Often at home when I have a pile of manuscripts to read and never enough time in the office to touch them, I get up in the night and skim through one or two while Lucas is sleeping.

I knew I would not be able to go back to sleep instantly; finally I decided to go downstairs and have a glass of milk and read some more Sherlock Holmes. I put on my robe and slippers and left without disturbing Lucas.

I was halfway down the hall when I realized I was heading for the plant room door. I turned and almost ran in the other direction. Never again, I thought. I would never go there again. I found the book where I had left it in the television room and took it to the kitchen where I got milk and a handful of cookies. I hesitated only a moment, then went to the bright breakfast room to read and nibble. Now and then the wind gusted; each time I found myself staring at the windows, almost afraid something would be torn loose out there, be hurled through the glass. After a while I realized I had read a page and could not recall anything on it. I felt even more tense than I had upstairs; I had eaten only part of one cookie and had not touched the milk. I drank it quickly, as if it were medicine, and took the glass out to rinse and put in the dishwasher. I remembered that I had left a trail of lights turned on behind me, and retraced my steps to switch them all off. At the stairs at the end of the hall, I stopped. There was still light coming from somewhere. The living room.

I had not gone into the living room. Someone else must have been having a sleepless night too. I started up the stairs and was stopped by the sound of a distant crash, followed by a resurgence of fear that something might blow through one of the windows. Reluctantly, I went to the living room doorway and glanced inside. No one was in sight.

No, I thought. No! There was another crash. Without thinking I ran through the room, up the stairs to the plant room, crying out now. "No! Stop it!" I felt sick with rage and fear. Plants were everywhere on the floor, pots smashed, upturned, dirt scattered. I saw no one. Whoever had done it had already left through the hallway door to the second floor of the house. I began to repot an African violet, weeping as I worked.

"Regina! What the hell is going on?"

"Regina? Are you all right?"

I looked up stupidly, blinded by the lights. Conrad and Hugh Froelich were entering the plant room from the hallway. They stopped together and stared at the mess.

"What have you done?" Conrad whispered. "My God, what have you done?"

"I . . . I didn't . . ." I looked from Conrad to my hands, covered with moist dirt. There was dirt on my robe where I had been kneeling.

"I know you didn't," Hugh Froelich said. "Come on. Let's get you cleaned up."

I couldn't stop staring at my hands as we all went back

to the kitchen, where Hugh held them under water, washed them. He brushed the dirt from my robe, and presently I was sitting down and Conrad was giving me a cup of coffee. If anyone talked until then, I can't remember. I had no memory of going into the breakfast room again. The few cookies I had taken out were still there, along with the Sherlock Holmes book.

"Can you tell us anything about it?" Hugh asked.

I shook my head. He was too tight, I kept thinking. Something in him was sure to break apart. Conrad pulled a chair close to mine and took my hand. I pulled it back, afraid some of the dirt would come off on him.

"I'm sorry I said you did it. Of course you didn't. Did you see anyone?"

I shook my head again.

"Why did you go up there?" he asked, keeping his voice soft and easy, not at all like the voice he had used with Janet.

I told them what I could. When I got to the part about noticing the light, I stopped. It had not been on before when I passed the doorway. I had not even considered that when I went back to look into the living room. I had passed that doorway twice; it had been closed and no light had shown.

"What is it?" Hugh asked. "You've remembered something?"

"Someone must have come down from the balcony into the living room and left the door open while I was turning off the other lights. I would have seen the light earlier if it had been on."

"No way," Hugh said. "If anyone had left that mess, there would have been a trail of dirt on the stairs, into the living room. There wasn't. I looked."

"Was there dirt going into the upstairs hallway?" Conrad asked, straightening up, as if getting ready to leave.

"For a few steps. Then whoever it was must have taken off the dirty shoes and carried them. That's why I knew she hadn't done it. I heard the door slam. It woke me up. We were in that plant room within a minute of the slamming of the door."

Conrad slumped back in his chair. "I guess I heard it too," he said. "I thought a tree had blown down. You can turn on the living room lamp from up there, by the way."

They both looked at me again. Hugh said, "Okay, you saw the light and you went to have a look. What then?"

I tried to remember, but it was confused. I remembered how moist and warm the potting soil was. "There was a crash, something breaking, and I realized it was something up on the balcony. I started to run up there. I don't know why. I think I yelled. And then you came in. I can't remember anything else." I found myself looking at my hands again.

"Why did you start repotting that thing?" Hugh asked gently.

"I don't know. I don't remember. It seemed such an evil thing, so cruel. I was mad and afraid . . ."

"You want more coffee?" Conrad asked, and now he was using the other voice, the dead voice that concealed him.

"She needs it," Hugh said. "Regina, your hands are all right. The dirt's gone."

I had been staring at them. I put them in my lap, but I could feel the dirt under my nails, under my ring. Conrad poured more coffee and sat down again.

"Drink it," Hugh said after a moment. I lifted the cup and sipped. "Don't you want cream?" he asked.

"Yes."

"What's the matter with her?" Conrad asked. I looked at him. He was studying my face.

"I think you'd better call Lucas," Hugh said. He took the cup from my hands, added cream, and gave it back to me. "Drink it," he said gently.

I had forgotten that Conrad was getting Lucas out of bed, and when they both entered the breakfast room, I thought it was morning, breakfast time. I didn't want Lucas to see my dirty hands, my dirty robe.

"Honey, what's wrong? What happened?" Lucas held my shoulders and examined my face, exactly the way Conrad had looked at me.

I started to tell him what I had told Hugh and Conrad, beginning at the same point, waking up to hear the wind, getting up, coming downstairs . . .

"I think we'd better call the doctor," Conrad said, breaking in.

"I agree," Hugh said. "You want to call? And then maybe we should have a look around."

Part Two

October 17, Continued

"REGINA IS IN a state of shock, not screaming or fainting or anything dramatic; it is rather as if she has gone cataleptic. She agrees to any suggestion without hesitation. Say talk and she talks; say sit down and she sits. Sizemore gave her a tranquilizer that was worthless; she is already tranquil. She is so pliant she has become like a rubber doll.

"I took her and Lucas to my house and left them there. Obviously she can't stay in the big house any longer."

Hugh Froelich turned off the tape recorder and stared at the notebook on his desk. He had made copies of the pages she had written since her arrival, had read them over twice, and he felt a sense of uneasiness that was almost physical, as if a cold were coming on, or something he had eaten had turned out to be poisonous.

"There is no mechanism for it," he said bitterly, with his finger on the record button, but not pushing it down. Hysteria could take many forms, he thought clearly. People don't have to have functional blindness, or paralysis, or anything overt. They can become docile and childlike, puttylike. He slammed his hand against the desktop in frustration. She was a pretty, healthy young woman, good features, good body. She was self-confident, self-contained, quiet, observant, smart, probably good at her job, efficient. Too thin, but he could not tell if that was the result of a deliberate diet, or heredity, or circumstances of the present. She was not the type, he thought again, to become hysterical. Finding that mess in the plant room should not have induced anything more than a mild shock, a transitory shock. And nothing more than that could have happened. She had interrupted someone in a destructive act, nothing more. There was no mechanism for anything more.

Grimly he read through the notebook again and then snapped it shut. She had written that no one had attended the funeral, but at least a hundred people had been there. Called as hastily as it had been, still a hundred people had shown up. Why had she written otherwise? And later, telling what happened, she said that the living room light had been on. He knew that was wrong; he had switched on the plant room light himself and before then everything had been dark. Not too dark for anyone whose eyes had adjusted, but not light either. She had not seen the living room light on, or else she had turned it off herself. He did not believe that, neither did he believe that she had run through the dark living room, up dark stairs, to repot the flowers, also in the dark. Someone else turned off the light, then. And she didn't notice?

He put the notebook and his copies into his briefcase and stalked from his office in the psych building without seeing anyone in the halls or on the stairs or in the parking lot. Normally he walked back and forth from his house to work and he was unfamiliar with the parking lot. He thought it unnecessarily jammed, but he liked the shade trees throughout it. Every year there was a battle over whether to cut the trees down to provide a few more parking spaces. He suspected that it was a rigged fight, staged only to still the protests over the inevitable parking crunch.

His house was on a small side street lined with horse chestnut trees that met overhead. They were not bare yet, although the ground was inches deep with leaves. Signs of autumn were everywhere, but still the pleasant weather held. His grass would need one last mowing, he thought, striding past it, forgetting it again. He had put off repainting the porch until now it was almost too late in the year to attend to it; if the weather changed, paint would take forever to dry and until then it would accumulate dust, twigs, whatever junk was in the air. He had his key out, but he hesitated and rang the bell instead. He had turned the house over to Regina and Lucas for as long as they wanted and for the duration his house was their house, their house his. Povertyville, he thought, after the big house they had left. Lucas finally opened the door.

"Any change?"

Lucas shook his head. "I think she's sleeping now. She was dozing a while ago. Mallory's on his way in."

Hugh nodded. "Mind if I make coffee?"

Lucas looked uncomfortable. "We probably will go to a hotel."

"She'll be better off here. I just thought Mallory might like a cup of coffee when he arrives." He didn't wait for a response, but went to the kitchen and busied himself grinding coffee, measuring water. Lucas followed miserably; he looked as if he should be sleeping too. He had been ill very recently, Hugh remembered, wondering if his recovery had been complete, if he was still convalescing. He didn't look well. And now he had to decide what to do next. Stay here with his wife or go back to the house and play a dead man's macabre game.

Mallory arrived before the coffee was ready. He looked angry and mean. Without preliminary he said to Lucas, "Now are you willing to get the hell out of here, go back home?"

"I can't," Lucas mumbled.

"You can. I called the airline. They're holding reservations for you."

"What about you?"

"When you're on that plane, I'm heading back home. And I'm getting another opinion about that goddam will. I intend to fight it all the way."

"Give everything to Conrad and Janet. They won't leave."

"You know damn well no one's going to win!"

"I don't even know for sure you'll take off if we go. For all I know you want to stay and try for it yourself!"

Mallory bunched his hands until his knuckles showed white. He turned and stamped out. He slammed the door hard.

"You're not taking her back there, are you?" Hugh asked.

Lucas gave him a dark look, as if he would like to resume trying to strangle him. "I'm hiring a nurse to come here and stay with her at night," he said. "I'll rent a car and come back later." He went into the bedroom, and Hugh, after a regretful glance at the coffee, started for the door. It was a nice little house, for the first time too little. He wanted to talk with Regina again, but not with Lucas there in his present mood. He wondered if Lucas had ever fought with Mallory before, had ever crossed him in any way. He remembered the notebook, took it from his brief-case, and put it on an end table. He wanted to ask her to continue to write in it, but maybe she didn't need any suggestion. It might even be better if he didn't bring it up, not raise the question about possible copies. He didn't want to have to deny that he had read it, or copied it, or anything else.

Driving back to the house he kept trying to apply his own advice to himself: You are not responsible for anyone else's state of mind. Yes he was, he kept thinking. He had not been very good at counseling; he always got impatient because the problems students became suicidal over always seemed so solvable. Stop seeing him. Give her up. Study harder. Don't smoke dope. One day his mentor, Dr. Fields, had said to him, stop counseling, and he had laughed out loud. So simple. He had been stewing about it for weeks, losing sleep, worrying before, during, and after every ses-sion. The one thing he always stressed with the students was: You are responsible for your actions, for your state of mental health as well as your physical health. And now that was going, just as almost everything he had ever be-lieved in seemed to become smoke when he really needed it. He was responsible. Those people out there in that house, waiting, dreading something, nurturing anxiety, watching it grow, fighting with each other, they had be-come his responsibility. That girl with her empty smile and pliant manner, he was responsible for her too. And Lucas, pale as a ghost, haggard, worried out of his mind over her, torn between duty to her and . . . what? money? a need to prove something? Whatever it was, he was re-sponsible for him. All of them.

Regina dozed, awakened, dozed again until late in the afternoon when she finally came wide awake. For a long time she could not remember where she was or why she was here. A double bed, a chest of drawers, a closet door slightly ajar . . . All so spartan and tidy. Where did he keep his junk? The things that just accumulated. Now she could hear the television dimly, and there was a coffee fragrance. She was very hungry. No one had given her breakfast or lunch, not even a snack, she thought ag-grievedly. That damn doctor had given her a capsule, and Conrad and Janet had sat with her on the couch . . . She shook her head; it all faded after that and the memories were strange, like a faintly seen film of someone she had not been very interested in.

She got up and put on her robe and went out to find Lucas. He was sprawled in a low chair before the television. He leaped to his feet at her appearance.

"Honey! Are you okay?"

She nodded. "Hungry. What time is it?"

He told her three-thirty and she blinked. A whole day gone. Maybe that was the only way to get through the rest of them, using the little, magic time capsules.

"I'll get you an egg and coffee and toast for now, and then you shower and dress and let's take a walk into town," Lucas said. "I'll buy a sketch pad, maybe some pencils; we'll rent a car and have a real dinner somewhere . . . Okay?"

She nodded, and for a moment she thought of the past week in New York. Their decision not to buy two pens at seventy-nine cents each. The way they always had to juggle sums like that. She was still paying off college loans, and he had gone into debt between jobs, just trying to stay alive. Such hardship back there, she thought bitterly, and such wealth out here. Her parents would have wanted to help, if they had known, but she had never told them. She knew they would have mortgaged their house to help her and she had lied to them about finances. And all the time *his* father had had so much.

She settled for coffee and toast. "Can we afford to pay for a car, dinner in town?" She glanced at the kitchen dubiously. "I could probably cook something."

"Mallory advanced me some cash," Lucas said. "Strohm said he'd put a check in a bank for us to use until the estate is settled." He sat across the table from her and played with a spoon. "What happened?" he asked suddenly. "Back at the house. What happened to you?"

She put down her cup and shook her head. "I told you. I told everyone. I don't know why I did anything. I don't remember what I thought or what I felt. Just what I did."

"But damn it! You had to think something! Why did you decide to go up there?"

"I don't know."

"Regina! For Christ's sake! Did you hear anyone up there? Did you hear voices?"

"I told you! I don't remember hearing anything but

crashes. Leave me alone. I'm going to shower and get dressed." She ran from the kitchen, and stood inside the bathroom with her back to the door, as if holding it shut. She closed her eyes and took a deep breath and exhaled it very slowly. She must not think about it. When she found herself trying to remember, she could feel a blankness settling over her, like a shot of Novocain in her mind. Leave me alone, she said under her breath. Just leave me alone! And she knew she meant more than Lucas; she meant the house, his father, whatever else was there that she could not name. Leave me alone, she said over and over silently.

Hugh prowled the grounds all afternoon under a drizzly sky that looked low enough to touch. He stood outside the sunroom windows and looked in at the bed where Regina had seen *him* the last time. The fuchsias dripped and he could imagine the slugs sampling the air, welcoming the change in the weather, eager for darkness. He looked up at the plant room, then down the lava road toward the bridge, not visible from here, where Lucas had watched his mother crash and die. He could imagine the truck roaring through the fields, beating her to the bridge. The road had become dark red, as if the rain had changed to blood. He turned away angrily from his own thoughts and went back inside.

"Oregon," Janet said, surveying him. "It's come back."

It had taken him a year to get used to the way people in Oregon walked around in the rain apparently without noticing it. No umbrellas, no hats, no scarfs. Not in the occasional hard rains, they were like other people then, but in the daily winter mist and drizzle and light rain that fell intermittently, or simply hung in the air, they acted as if the sun were shining, went about their business and got wet, or at least very moist. After that first year, he had found that he was doing exactly the same thing, out without an umbrella or hat because either would have been a waste of time and a burden and not very necessary. No one got very wet, but no one was entirely dry most of the winter either. His former wife never had got used to it. Such weather, she used to say, made a mockery out of the best hairdresser.

He ran his hands through his hair; just a little damp,

but Janet was right, Oregon had come back after a long dry summer.

"They're having drinks in the television room whenever you want to join them," Janet said, heading for the stairs.

"Thanks," he said. As soon as she was out of sight on the staircase, he went instead to the living room. It looked naked without the greenery up there. The light looked different; he had become used to the green filter effect. Anita Mantessa had cleaned up everything and no plants remained. He remembered the night he had come to dinner four years ago. The first time he had seen Culbertson he had been up there, outlined against the windows, a trowel in one hand, a potted plant in the other. He had been a large man, big chested, broad, although his legs had been thin and a little short for his body. Not misshapen, but not classically proportioned either. His head had been large, made to appear even larger by his fluffy hair, which stood out in an aureole.

"Froelich, are you? Read your paper. Don't believe in possession, eh? Neither do I. Neither do I," he had said. There was an elevator chair on the rail; he rode it down, saying a slick salesman had talked him into trying it. A short while ago, thinking he might have had a stroke, he had become alarmed enough to have an EEG made. The problem had turned out to be an inner-ear infection caused by sinus trouble, he had said. Then he had touched Hugh's chest and pushed slightly. "Don't believe in coincidence, either, sir. One month after Sizemore had that thing made I read your article, and I thought, aha, that's why I had it done. Funny, don't you think?" He laughed, a strange sound, like the rattle of dry sticks or bones.

Hugh, looking up the stairs, could almost see him again, gliding down without touching the rail, a black shadow that grew larger and larger. Larger now than ever, he thought. He could understand why the Culbertson children, grown men and a grown woman, still feared and hated him. All his life he had gotten everything he ever set out after, everything. He had said that himself, and Hugh had believed and believed even more after looking him up in the newspaper files and asking questions about him around the campus and in town. Nothing he had wanted had ever been denied him. Last spring he had announced what he was going after next, laughing but not crazy. Oh, no, not crazy at all.

"Tell me why you're convinced it can't happen," he had said that last night. "Oh, not that technical brain-as-a-machine part, but your own beliefs. All the rest is just a way to shore up your own beliefs. I want to know what your standing ground is, what the hell you're shoring up."

Hugh had taken a deep breath, angry with the old man and his scorn, his arrogance. "You know we have to learn how to use our senses? The infant learns how to see, how to interpret the signals, for instance." The old man nodded impatiently. "Okay. Along with the usual senses we all admit to, we develop another one that says, *I am.* Call it self, self-consciousness, ego, whatever you like. It will fight to maintain its integrity. It can't simply step aside and stop existing because it's a product of the cortex. It comes into being with the development of the cortex and as long as the cortex functions, this sense of *I am* endures. Powerful drugs, severe injury to the cortical area, or death can stop it, but nothing else can. No one can impose his sense of sight on you, make you see through his eyes. If I touch a stove, you can't feel it. Imagining it is as close as you can come. You have senses that see, hear, taste, feel, touch, and one that says *I am.* They are equally inviolable."

"What about hypnosis? Conversion?"

"Two different things. Conversion is an abrupt change of belief systems. It is still *I* who believes. We believe any number of different things in a lifetime, but the *I am,* the ego, if you prefer, is the same. And under hypnosis the subject is in an altered state of suggestibility. He will act on the hypnotist's suggestions as long as they are acceptable. If they are not acceptable, he can come out of trance —the usual response—reinterpret them, go into actual sleep, or ignore them. Which one he chooses is determined by personality factors. The sense of *I am,* the ego, is never really at risk. It has too many defenses."

"Delusions," Culbertson said, laughing. The laugh turned into a cough that seemed to be strangling him.

Hugh started to go find Greta. The old man waved him down again. "Delusions," he repeated, hardly above a whisper. "I am, we are. It is. I'll have to find the weak spots in their defenses, won't I, Professor?"

Greta had come in then. "It's late," she had said, dismissing Hugh.

This time when he stood up, no one motioned him to stay any longer.

"I still don't believe in it," Culbertson had said, in his hoarse whisper. "That's for the record, and it's true. If it can happen, I'll do it. You don't have to believe. If you experience it, you know. I am," he said, his voice fading. "I am. It's a lie, Professor. It's a lie."

Hugh shook himself back to the present. "There is no mechanism," he said aloud, and for a moment he could almost hear that dry, rattling laugh. He went to join the others in the television room. He could use a drink, he thought, hurrying.

He was rushing even faster from his own thoughts, his answer to the question about why they were all there. The children had no choice. Culbertson had known that exactly as Hugh had known it. Their reaction to his terms had been as predictable as any freshman stimulus-response experiment with a white rat. Dr. Fields had told Hugh no one would force him to conduct such a ridiculous experiment. The medical department could easily make the EEGs and keep them on file, and one of the neurologists could make the comparisons. He could have been out from the beginning. Yet here he was, and Culbertson had known he would be here.

"You'll stay," he had whispered that night. "You'll be here from start to finish."

Curiosity? Vindication for the paper that actually had been rather tongue-in-cheek, although Culbertson had not read it like that? Whatever it was, he would stay; he paused before the door to the television room. Behind the door, Mallory was cursing in a booming voice. Hugh hoped Mallory would never try to strangle him. It was almost a certainty that he would succeed.

He had been threatened, he thought then. In some way that he had not yet examined closely, he had been seriously threatened. And, as much as his instincts urged him to flee, to take cover, his rational self demanded that he stay and even participate in this insanity.

"Ask him," Conrad drawled as Hugh entered. He was in one of the leather chairs, his long legs stretched out before him. Hugh remembered Regina's mention of his feet in her journal. Size thirteen at least.

Mallory gave him a bitter look and sat down opposite

his brother. "Isn't it possible that Ginny did it, all of it, herself?"

"Remotely possible," Hugh admitted.

Mallory glanced at Conrad. "She, for God alone knows what reason, went up there and smashed everything. She started through the hallway back to her room and maybe the door slammed behind her, waking her up. She could have been sleepwalking or something. She realized what she had done and went back and tried to undo it. As simple as that. Of course, she doesn't remember doing it in the first place, not if she was sleepwalking."

"And the book? The cookies? The glass in the dishwasher? Sleepwalking?" Conrad didn't look at Mallory and didn't raise his voice above the sleepy drawl. He glanced at Hugh. "We went through all the rooms looking for dirty shoes. Didn't find anything. Didn't really expect to. Plenty of time to clean up. There were gloves up there in that mess, could have fit any of us."

Mallory dismissed the snack and the book. "Who knows how many times she was up and down?"

"Maybe," Hugh said. He mixed himself a drink and noticed that soda and ginger ale now appeared along with the assortment of liquors. That did simplify it, he decided. She could have become so upset over Lucas's story of life in the old homestead that she had acted out her resentment and anger for his father, taking it out on his plants. Asleep or awake, she could have done it, and she most certainly would have denied it later if she remembered.

He knew that Conrad didn't believe that, and neither did he. No one who had been with her in the hour after they had found her would believe it.

Janet came in and said that dinner was ready. No plate had been set for Lucas. Janet had a large salad and a piece of broiled fish; the others had lamb chops in a rich velvety sauce. Dinner was a silent meal. Afterward they all returned to the television room where Conrad watched an old movie, Janet did her needlepoint, and Mallory went over a ledger, making notes, flipping pages back and forth. Hugh had brought a pile of journals that had been accumulating. His department head was leaning on him more than usual these days to publish, but he generally hated the journals, primarily because of the jargon. Papers on the visual cortex, on Broca's area, on the cellular structure of the myelin sheath . . . It was like studying the fabric and metals that made up an automobile, and never guessing what the entire structure was for. He read a White and Lieberman paper on their latest work with the split brain phenomenon, and even that left him dissatisfied. They needed a new approach. An Einsteinian break-through into a new way of thinking, or perceiving what was there. A holistic approach that considered the entire organ, not its various parts that never could be made to add up to the whole. They kept milking the same tired cow, he thought with irritation, turning pages faster, bored with one paper after another. And the cow was running dry, although no one seemed to notice. Cow runs dry, you slaughter it, if it's too old to breed again, he thought, and the page he was staring at seemed to waver out of focus. He jerked. He had nearly fallen asleep; he glanced about to see if anyone had noticed. Conrad was still watching the television and, across the room, Mallory was regarding the ceiling with a frown wrinkling his forehead. Janet was threading a needle.

"Seven hundred eighty-five acres of prime Douglas fir," Mallory murmured. "I thought that had been sold years ago."

Conrad glanced at him, back to the movie.

"Wonder what it's going for now," Mallory said.

"Five hundred a thousand board feet," Conrad replied without turning.

Hugh was sitting fairly close to Conrad, almost facing him. He saw the sudden start that rippled through his long, lank body, saw his fingers tighten on the arms of his chair.

Conrad stared at the television fixedly; his jaw tightened until a bulge appeared; after a moment he relaxed and took a deep breath. He closed his eyes, and when he opened them, he was normal in appearance. Hugh, pre-tending to read, flipped a page before he looked at Con-rad, who was watching him.

"Fix you a drink?" Conrad asked in his sleepy voice.

"Thanks. Have they cut that movie much? I saw it years ago and it was pretty good."

"Tell the truth," Conrad said, "I haven't been paying much attention." He made the drinks and ambled out of the room, leaving the set on. Janet got up and switched it off.

"What happened to him?" she whispered. "You saw, didn't you?"

Hugh shrugged. "I don't know."

Janet glanced at the liquor but did not approach it. Sitting down again she picked up her handiwork. "I read your article this afternoon. You really do believe it's impossible, don't you?"

"Yes. Absolutely."

"And telepathy, precognition, all the ESP effects, they're impossible too?"

"I believe so. It's coincidence. How many times do we all have hunches that are wrong? We forget them. But no one ever forgets the one in a thousand that turns out to be right. Hunches can be explained by everyday normality."

She smiled slightly. "Let me tell you about a coincidence I experienced years ago," she said. "I was twenty, studying art under Rudolf Fiske. You know his work at all?"

Hugh nodded. "Modernist, abstract stuff?"

"That's the one. I liked abstract art for a while. That's all I was doing. Not very well because I have very little talent. He never looked at our work until we were ready to show him. At this time I was working on something quite different from my usual stuff. I had been at it for three weeks when one day one of the students went crazy and jumped out the window. I didn't know him; he had just come into the class during the last week. I had never seen him before that. I became hysterical and Rudolf slapped me. I couldn't speak. Finally he looked at my painting. It was that student as he must have looked down there on the pavement, staring at the sky, splashed out in all directions. His face was quite recognizable. There was green paint on his hands—in the painting and down there on the street."

She stopped talking; her needle slipped into the canvas, out again, trailing a light-blue thread. Hugh took a deep breath, but before he could speak, she said, without looking up, "Don't say you believe, or disbelieve, or that it was coincidence, or anything else."

He exhaled. She was right. There was never anything to say. It had happened just as she had told it, or nothing had happened, or something had happened and she had distorted it.

"Has anything else like that ever happened to you?" he asked finally.

"Not just like that. Nothing dramatic or exciting. A few little things, but I won't bore you with them. Even I could see how they might be called coincidences, although, of course, they weren't."

She looked at him still smiling faintly, and for a moment he saw the beauty that Regina had seen, lovely eyes, very fine complexion. Then it was gone and again she was simply an immensely overweight woman. She turned her attention once more to her needlework. He felt uncomfortable, as if she knew he had seen her, really seen her, however briefly, and that he had not been able to maintain the image. When had she started to put on weight, he wondered. At twelve, when her father had beaten her because she had kissed her half-brother, or gone further than a kiss perhaps? And now, at thirty-five—virginal, no matter what had happened then, she was virginal—was she going to try to catch up with the life that she had missed for so many years? How long would it take to lose seventy-five pounds? A year? Two years? His thoughts were interrupted by the arrival of Lucas. It was nearly midnight.

He stood in the doorway and said good night.

"Luke, wait a minute. I'm going up, too," Janet said, dropping her work into the basket by her chair. They went out together, speaking in low tones. The closing of the door silenced their voices completely; again Hugh was reminded of the solidity of the house where no noise carried beyond any door.

"Me too," Mallory said. He stood up, leaving the ledger open, a pencil between the pages. He went to the door, where he paused. "I'm leaving my bedroom door cracked tonight. Would you mind leaving yours open a little, just in case . . ."

"I intended to," Hugh said, and Mallory nodded, said good night, and left the room. He looked old and tired, as if his quarrel with Lucas had hurt him more than the death of his father. Or it could have been the cumulative effect of the death, funeral, fight, the insane will . . . Or maybe it was because he didn't believe any more than Hugh did that Regina had destroyed the plants. But if she had not done it, then one of them had. No one else had been in the house overnight. Anita Mantessa and her husband lived in a small cottage up the lava road, and Greta had already left. One of the children, or Regina or Hugh.

He sat before the fire for another half-hour before he

closed the screen and switched off lamps in the room. He paused at the desk and looked at the ledger without real curiosity. He knew the valley was full of people who were land-poor, all their wealth tied up in the acreage that they couldn't bring themselves to divide. It seemed almost a condition of the farmers here: They fell in love with the rich land and accumulated more and more of it until their taxes were too burdensome. Only then did they begin to strip it off again. He was afraid the Culbertson children would be bitterly disappointed when they learned the extent of the other assets.

"I'm a wealthy man," Culbertson had said during that first meeting. "Not cash, never's enough cash. But rich in what counts, the only thing that counts. Land. Funny thing about land is the more you think you own, the more it owns you. It's alive, the land is. It's a mystical thing I'm talking about, sir, something you psychologists can't acknowledge, I know. But it's a real thing I'm talking about. You touch that land out there and you touch something that's living, breathing, touching back. You'd think of all my children at least one of them would understand that, wouldn't you? They don't. Land is negotiable for them, and that's all it is. Even Mallory, who owns a couple of thousand acres of scrub, he doesn't realize it's something more than a way to make more money. It's a way to live, a master to serve as long as you live, a home to go to after you live."

How could anyone with that kind of love in him show so much hatred for people, for his own children, his wives? Hugh turned off the desk lamp and left the room. He started through the living room toward the curved staircase to the upper hall, then stopped and instead went on to the stairs everyone else always used. He felt foolish, but he didn't even try to unravel the reason for disliking that room, those stairs, that balcony. He knew he had no reason.

October 18

LUCAS ARRIVED at the little house the next morning at seven-thirty. He looked wretched, as if he had not slept. He held Regina tightly, then drew back to look at her. "How are you? Where's the nurse?"

"Okay. I sent her away. She snored like a trooper all night. And ate like one this morning. I won't stay here alone again, Lucas. We stay together here, or there, or at home, wherever."

He took a deep breath, as if preparing to argue with her, and she turned her back on him and went into the kitchen. "I have coffee made if you want some." She stopped at the table and held on to it with both hands. "Lucas, let's go home. Today. This morning. You'll have the cash, that's enough." She did not look at him and when the silence lengthened, she found that she was gripping the table harder and harder.

Finally he said, "You know that's impossible."

"Why is it?"

His voice was angry now, the words fast, almost slurred. "I won't give up anything, not a cent of it! Do you understand? I was forced to pay my dues, Regina, and I won't give it up. Not for you, or myself, not for anything. All those years I paid, now I collect. That's why it's impossible. You go back. I wanted you to get out from the start."

She shook her head and now she released the grip that was making her hands ache. "Together," she murmured. "What will we do all day?"

She looked at him, and she knew it was not the money,

59

that wasn't his reason. He never had cared about money; if they had it, he spent it without a thought. When they were broke, he was patient, never complaining. He never had shown any urgency about money; even the game he played—When I Get Rich . . . —was without urgency. She knew it was not the inheritance as such that held him, and it was frightening to think that he was trying to prove something to his father even now. You can't win, she wanted to say to him, echoing what Mallory had said. It's a no-win game. You can't prove a point to a dead man; he can't prove anything to you.

Lucas was rigid, too ready to make the argument into a real fight. Regina knew she dared not let it go that far; a real fight would require time to sort out, hours of talk time, hours of making love time, the kind of time they did not have and would not have until they were away from the farm and the insane conditions of the will. Last night the sedative the doctor had given her had put her to sleep easily, but she had come awake in the middle of the night, and, sitting up in Hugh's bed, she had felt herself being pulled back, stretched out between the town and the farm-house, had felt herself reaching out to touch Lucas at her side. A dream, she knew; nothing but a silly dream, but it had left her uneasy, unwilling to be separated from him again at night, unwilling to have him alone in that house. His family did not count, she knew. He was alone unless she was with him, just as she was alone without him, no matter how crowded the scenes each moved through. She took a deep breath. They could not fight now, not until next week sometime. It was enough to make her smile— scheduling their next fight. Lucas smiled back at her and reached out to put his arms around her.

"I love you," he whispered. "Ever tell you that?"

"You hinted from time to time."

"Let's go to bed before we make any demanding decisions."

Hugh was ready to leave the big house for campus to check in at his office when Lucas and Regina drove up in the rental car. He met them at the door.

"We're going to go look for fossils," Regina said. "Lucas has some petrified wood from up the stream somewhere. He remembers where it came from. I've never seen any in the wild."

Too voluble, Hugh thought. Too determinedly not looking around the house.

"I'll go up and get my old backpack," Lucas said. "And
some rain gear for you. You may need it before the day is
over. Anything else?"

She shook her head. "Can't think of a thing." Lucas ran
up the stairs and she said to Hugh, "It's a beautiful day."

"You should have stayed in town."

She frowned, then turned and opened the door, looked
out. "I was upset. It scared me for someone to make such
a mess. I'm fine now. Besides, Lucas hasn't been back
here for years; it was killing him not to see some of the
old places he used to know."

"Do you remember what happened to you? How you
were afterward?"

"Scared," she said again. "We're not staying here more
than a minute or two. We have lunch stuff with us. Being
in the woods will do us both good." She did not add that
no decision had been made yet about the night.

Conrad appeared on the stairs yawning and stretching.
"Saw Lucas. How're you, Regina?"

"Good. We're going fossil hunting."

"So he said. Mind if I tag along? Been years since I was
out in the woods."

She hesitated only a moment before she said, with ap-
parent sincerity, "I was hoping you'd want to come. Lucas
says you were the one who always found them."

"I can dowse, too," Conrad said, grinning. "Course, I'm
pretty careful who I tell that to. Be a minute. Just grab a
quick bite, ask Anita for some lunch, and be ready. Mind
waiting a minute or two?"

She shook her head, smiling back at him, and he went
down the hallway toward the breakfast room. Regina
glanced at Hugh.

"Weren't you on your way out?"

"Not really. I could use more coffee."

They followed Conrad. As they passed the living room
door, Regina said, "I really don't have to be watched, you
know. I didn't do anything."

"I know."

Abruptly she stopped and faced him squarely. "Listen,
Hugh Froelich, we think, Lucas and I, that you're the one
who should leave. We don't like being under observation
all the time. I don't like it."

"I'm not watching you," he said stiffly. "I'm concerned about you, about all of you."

"Don't waste it on us. You must have work to do in town." She moved on ahead of him, going quickly to the breakfast room.

Hugh followed, puzzled by the change in her, the assertiveness that he had not noticed before. He found himself wishing he had known them all before this; there was nothing to compare them to, no way of knowing if the changes he saw in them were regressive or progressive, adaptive or damaging. Was this the real Regina, determined, unafraid, protective? He nodded to himself at that. She was being protective of Lucas and that meant she thought he needed protection in his father's house. How furious she would be if she could track his thoughts now.

Mallory was eating, reading the morning paper. He said good morning and kept reading. Regina looked confused; Hugh wondered if she knew anything about the brief argument between Lucas and his brother. "It's going to rain," he said, going to the windows. Low mist hung over the hills, truncated the mountains.

"Not till late afternoon," Conrad said. "We'll be back before it starts."

In a moment Lucas joined them and they all had coffee while Mallory continued to read his paper. He didn't turn the page, Hugh noticed. Conrad ate little, and he ate quickly; within ten minutes he announced that he was game if they were.

Hugh watched them move across the field, turn to follow the river up into the hills. Regina was very small between the two men. She was wearing a red sweater and jeans and looked like a young boy as the three figures vanished behind trees.

Mallory was standing at the windows, also watching. "That goddam fool!" He went back to his chair and sat down heavily. "You hear anything during the night?"

"Nothing. You?"

"No. I was afraid I had slept pretty deeply, though. I was beat."

He still looked beat. There were circles under his eyes, a dirty, grayed-yellow color, as if both eyes had been hurt and were just beginning to show the bruises.

Hugh left for his office soon after that. There were no letters that were worth opening and nothing from his TA.

One phone call to return. Laura. He wished he had not come in at all. Laura. She had called last night and again this morning. If he had stayed at the farm he wouldn't have known she called and he wouldn't have to struggle with his conscience again, and he was damn sick and tired of the never-ending struggle. His hand reached for the phone even as he considered ignoring her messages. He dialed.

Her voice wrenched him the way it always had; she stimulated a pinched nerve that triggered a mental spasm; that was how he thought of it.

"Hello, Laura," he said evenly. "I'm returning your calls."

"Are you all right, Hugh? When you didn't call back last night, I was so worried. Who is that woman in our house?"

"My house, Laura. I'm letting her and her husband use it for a while. Did you want something?"

He looked out his window at a dark spruce tree that was over a hundred years old and nearly two hundred feet tall. He admired that tree enormously. It was the essence of spruce. Usually when he thought things like that he was stoned, or drunk, or talking to Laura. She went on about her concern for him, that he had not been home, on and on. She was lonely, she said. Maybe she would run up for a visit, only a few days.

"No, Laura. Don't. I'm very busy." He closed his eyes and swung his chair back to his desk away from the spruce so it would not see his shame. She reminded him of the good years, of her true love, of his love that had failed them. Her voice was lovely, soft and melodious. She ended up asking him for a loan, just five hundred for three weeks.

After he hung up he leaned back with his eyes closed, in spite of himself going back over some of the good times, the very good times; in spite of himself going over some of the terrible times too. Then he wrote out the check, put it in an envelope and addressed it to her in Los Angeles where she was a partner in a specialty apparel shop, making as much money in six months as he made in a year. That had been part of it, he thought, but just a small part of it. The other part had been that his love had failed them, and that was the big part of it.

Most people simply separate, he thought, staring at the envelope, but after you've been married for nine years, separation isn't really all that final. John Daniel Culbert-

son, on the other hand, had managed a very permanent
separation from three wives in a row. He sighed, glanced
again at his desk for something else to occupy him, and,
finding nothing, reluctantly got up and left, carrying the
envelope which he deposited in the mail slot in the hall.
Nothing to do in town, might as well head back to the old
homestead, he thought, and he found that he didn't want
to go back. Not then, not ever. He didn't want to be there
when . . . When what? For a moment he had had a feeling that he knew exactly what it was he didn't want to face,
but it was gone again.

He walked slowly, nodding to people he knew. What a
strange thing for him to have thought of last night. When
the milk runs out you slaughter the cow if it's too old to
breed again. He had grown up in San Francisco and Hart-
ford, had gone to school at Columbia, had never lived on
a farm or visited a farm in his life until he had moved
here and had been summoned by John Daniel Culbertson.
What did he know about cows? That was the sort of thing
the old man might have said, he thought, and he stopped
five feet short of his car.

Regina watched Lucas climb the steep river bank and pull
himself up over the top. She let her breath out when he
was finished.

"You don't have to worry about him, you know," Conrad said gently. "He grew up climbing these hills."

She nodded. "It's so beautiful up here. It looks un-
touched, as if no one ever came here before today."

They had followed the rapid stream into the foothills
and for an hour they had been going upward through immense Douglas fir trees. Sometimes they stayed at the edge
of the stream, then they lost it, only to come across it
again, always wilder, whiter, faster than before. It was very
narrow here, and shallow, foamy, with the constant voice
of muted thunder. It was as if the stream could not contain
itself; its impatience to leave the mountain solitude sent it
leaping through the forest, hurling itself over cliffs, pausing
occasionally to get its bearings in a deceptively quiet pool
before it plunged again toward the nearest way down.

Glowing moss covered the trees, the rocks, and at the
edge of the stream there was a tangle of berry bushes:
salmonberries, blackberries, wineberries. The river was cut-

ting a gorge here, exposing strata of black earth three feet deep, five feet . . .

"On the way down we'll have to poke around for fossilized wood," Conrad said. "We've come up too high already. It's one of the biggest beds of fossilized wood in the world, and it's all buried, in some places as deep as twenty-five feet."

They had stopped to let Regina rest, and Conrad had admitted sheepishly that he was not good for much more climbing that day. They both watched Lucas scamper over the rocks like a boy.

"I don't understand why it turned to fossils in this climate," Regina said. "You'd think anything left out would rot almost overnight."

"It was different during the ice ages," Conrad said. "There was a climatic change, dry cold air killed everything and for thousands of years there was no life here. Then the thaw, and mud came sliding down the hills, covering it all. The valley was a giant inland sea, dammed with an ice dam, collecting silt for decades, hundreds of years, building up some of the deepest alluvial soil in the world. Finally the dam melted, the valley was drained, and in time the trees moved back in and hid all traces of the previous forests. What we hardly ever think about is the fact that the earth has all the time in the world to fix itself, repair whatever damage there is. It's only us, poor short-lived humans, who have no time."

Lucas came back to them, flushed and sweaty. "Let's go down a little lower and find some sun to sit in and eat lunch."

They began to pick their way back down. There was no trail, although Conrad said there had been one when he had lived in the big house. Already the forest had obliterated it. Again Lucas moved nimbly ahead apparently with no need to hunt for the best way down. "The instincts of a mountain goat," Conrad said, using a tree for support as he clambered down a ten-foot drop, then turned to help Regina. Lucas was far ahead of them, standing motionless.

They drew near him and Regina stopped also. They had come to a clearing of smooth rocks. Through the trees and over the lower forest slopes, they could see the farm, toylike trucks, miniature tractors. Slowly Regina walked to the edge of the smooth rocks. It was breathtaking, almost as if she were floating above the beautiful farmhouse, the lovely gardens. He had planned it all from up here, she thought suddenly, and she knew that was not altogether wrong. He had planned it in such a way that no matter where anyone stood to look it was perfection. Like a fairyland, a dreamscape . . .

"You can't get away from it," Lucas said bitterly and turned to sit on the rocks that looked almost polished. "Let's eat."

The sun was warm, but even as they watched, clouds began to meet, grow, cover the sky, starting with the western horizon, moving inland, joining clouds that already had formed over the mountains.

"He used to patrol the stream," Conrad said, looking at the sky. "Once he found a beer can, and he called out the farm hands, gave them a tongue-lashing. Said if it happened again, he'd fire the lot of them. I don't think it ever happened again."

Regina shivered. On the way up Conrad had told her that his father had bought the mountain just to have the source of the river, where it came gushing out of the earth. Volcanic water, Conrad called it. If it was going to live on his land, it had to be pure, uncontaminated.

"He believed in punishment," Lucas said. "Instant punishment. Did your father ever whip you?" he asked Regina.

She shook her head. "Dad seems to think life is hard enough without adding any unhappiness that can be avoided."

Conrad shrugged. "It really doesn't seem to matter to kids—punishment, no punishment—just as long as the parent is consistent. He was consistent. And fair enough, I think."

Lucas jumped up and deliberately tossed part of his sandwich over the rocks into the water below. The sunlight on his face accentuated the hollows under his eyes, under the sharp bones on his cheeks. He was so thin, looked so tired. He had not slept the night before, Regina knew. He had not really slept well since they left their New York apartment.

"Punishment's okay," Lucas said. "You deserve it, you get it. That's okay." He started to examine the rocky side of the clearing. "It's when you deserve it and don't get it and find yourself waiting and waiting . . . That's when it isn't fair. If you're going to be whipped, or sent to bed hungry, or whatever, it should just happen and be done with." He had found a way down and began to descend.

Regina stood up, no longer wanting to sit still and eat. "We should go back," she said. "It's going to rain."

She went to the edge of the rocks and looked down at Lucas who was midway to the stream below where there was a narrow bank, the boiling water, boulders, and then a small pool of quiet water, and a longer drop to the next pool. She remembered seeing it on the way up: a high narrow waterfall where it was impossible to talk over the roar of crashing water. She began to stuff things into the backpack Conrad had brought. Lucas had the other one. Conrad was in no hurry; he lighted another cigarette, still looking at the sky that was almost solidly overcast now.

"I'll start down," Regina said and hurried away, not over the side the way Lucas had gone, but along the same route they had used before, slower, not so steep. She was almost running by the time she reached the top of the next pool. The water here was calm, hardly even whispering, ten feet below the place where she came out. And there was Lucas ahead of her, moving steadily, not down toward the pool, but straight ahead where the trees ended on a cliff over a two-hundred-foot drop into a jumble of rocks and boulders and a churning basin. She could hear the water again as it rushed over the ledge, dropped, thundered at the bottom. Now the rain suddenly started to fall. There was no preliminary shower, no sprinkling, just a hard rain falling straight down as if it had been doing it for hours.

"Lucas!" Regina yelled. "Wait!"

Already the footing was treacherous, the mosses slick, the rocks coated with a film of mud. Lucas kept walking; he might not have heard her. She called again and ran, slipping, and screamed his name. She caught his arm and together they fell over the edge of the bank to the icy pool ten feet below, sliding all the way.

Regina lay with her lower legs in the water, her cheek in the mud, both hands clutching earth and rocks. Lucas had fallen in farther than she had. He was pulling himself from the water, dragging one leg.

"Are you all right?" he gasped. There was a long cut on his cheek. Blood ran down from it, followed the angle of his chin.

"Let me just get my breath," she said. Beyond him she could see the lip of the waterfall, the top of trees; the roar of water seemed to fill her head.

And then Conrad was there hauling her up and out of the water, settling her against a tree while he got Lucas pulled up.

"Is it broken?" he asked, feeling Lucas's leg. Lucas flinched and sank down to the earth with his leg outstretched. Conrad pulled his jeans leg up and looked at his knee. The rain was beating, ice cold, and now the woods and sky were all one, all gray, dripping.

"I'll splint it," Conrad said finally. "We'll have to get you down. Take too long to go for help, get back up here. You'd freeze in this rain."

He searched for a sapling as he talked. Regina kneeled before Lucas and wiped the cut on his cheek. He looked past her, his eyes narrowed in pain.

"I'm sorry," she whispered. "Lucas, I'm sorry." He did not look at her.

Conrad returned with two sticks and she moved out of the way and watched him splint the leg, immobilizing it at the knee.

"Will you get our rain gear out?" he asked. "And I guess you'll have to manage his backpack. Or we'll just leave it here and get it later."

She pulled out the ponchos, got one on Lucas, slipped on the pack and adjusted straps, and then pulled a poncho over her head. In a few minutes they were ready to descend. Where they could manage it, they moved three abreast and, although Lucas tried not to put any weight on Regina, he could not help but lean, and very quickly she was breathing hard. Her legs began to feel leaden. Where there was too little room for them all, she dropped behind, and at those times Conrad half carried his brother, staggering slightly, using trees where he could for balance and support. It was a nightmare trip through the rain, sliding down the steep hills. In the beginning Lucas had tried to use his injured leg, but more and more he was dragging it, and he was so pale Regina expected him to pass out long before they could reach the farm.

If they could just get out of the hills, she thought, they could stop and let Conrad go ahead for help. When she suggested it, Conrad shook his head. "More afraid of hypothermia than I am of hurting his leg any more," he said. His breath was coming in broken gasps and he was stopping frequently to rest. They were all soaked by then, but the rain was lighter as they made their way down toward the valley.

Mallory was the only one who could run the farm, Hugh thought, watching Mallory and another man who he supposed was Carlos Mantessa, the manager. They were walking away from the outbuildings; from a distance Mallory even resembled his father. More than any of the others, at any rate. The resemblance was in his build, in his broad heavy chest and thick arms, and the set of his head. From this window he had seen Bill Strohm and a stranger walking by, and he had remembered that today Culbertson's ashes were to be scattered on his farm, and that Strohm was to be a witness. Now, in death, the old man was still everywhere, keeping watch. He wished the rain would come and wash the damn ashes down the river, out to sea.

The two men were lost to sight around the corner of the house, and Hugh went back to the book he was reading; he was in the library in the alcove of a bow window. The afternoon light was failing as the clouds deepened; the rain would start soon. It had started already in the mountains. He wished the three hikers would get back. From where he sat he couldn't see the hall door, and Janet was well into the room before he realized it. She went to the wall of occult books and replaced two, withdrew two others, turned, and only then saw him at the window.

"He was a reader from as early as I can remember," she said, approaching him. She sat in the companion chair to his. "Was he crazy?"

"I don't think so. Do you?"

"I don't know. I used to think so when I was very young. I thought he was Bluebeard, or Jack the Ripper, or something like that for a long time. Then I decided he was psychopathic. Then I decided I couldn't judge him. I think he had his own moral code, not like anyone else's, but he stuck to it."

Hugh waited. She was using him as a sounding board. It happened quite often with students, too; they came in diffidently, with terrible decisions to make, in need of someone who would listen and not tell them what to do. He was good at that—not telling anyone what to do. His solutions were the sort that would enrage the students, and he had enough sense to understand at least that much. He waited for Janet to continue. Presently she did.

"He really hated women. All women. And yet he needed a woman at all times. That's the key to him. If you don't know that you'll never understand him at all."

"A lot of people feel a great deal of ambivalence about the opposite sex. It's built into our culture," Hugh said.

She shook her head vehemently. "Not like that. The way you sometimes look at me, that's the way he always looked at women. He always saw only the ugliness in them."

Hugh stifled his protest. Today she was wearing a caftan of navy blue, with a white scarf at her throat. Seated, shadowed, with only her face clear, she looked quite pretty. He had counseled overweight women at school, and he had some understanding of the agonies they suffered, the contempt they endured. His real advice, seldom voiced, had been to lose weight. Now he felt shame for his oversimplified solution to their problems.

"He hated me more than other women, because I was his daughter, and he was sure that I was even more evil, worse in every way, than his various wives. It wasn't the way any of them looked," she said pensively. "Luke's mother was very beautiful. I always wondered what he saw when he looked at her. Not what I saw." She seemed ready to get up and leave.

"You seem to understand him better than the others," Hugh said slowly, almost afraid he would drive her away if he even suggested a question.

"I studied him more than they did," she admitted. "I caught on early to the fact that he was puritanical about sex, for example. And obsessive about beautiful objects and people. Women, anyway. He paid for the remodeling of my house, you know. I was broke. I have no skills and I never finished enough education even to teach. Anyway, I decided I had to sell my house—my grandmother left it to me—and I called in a realtor. The next thing I knew an attorney was there talking to me about dividing it into apartments, renting out most of it, all that. I laughed in his face. You know how much just the plumbing would have cost? He said the money was available. If my mother had lived, she would have come into money, eventually I would have had it. I could have it then for that purpose. I understood that, too. Blood money. He was paying me off for the loss of a mother. Probably he was afraid I might someday ask if I could come back, if things got too tough. And he couldn't stand to look at me. I took the money." She stood up, looking out the window.

"They're coming back. Lucas is hurt!"

Hugh ran ahead of Janet to meet them. Conrad was supporting Lucas, who was very pale; there was a long cut on his cheek, and he was shivering hard, dripping wet.

Hugh draped Lucas's other arm over his shoulders and took half the weight and slowly they went on to the house. "What happened?"

"Fell down a bank into the river," Conrad said. He was breathing heavily. Hugh wondered how far he had walked half-carrying Lucas. "Nothing serious, I don't think. Sprained knee maybe."

Regina looked ghastly, very frightened, muddy, and bedraggled. "It's my fault," she said. "It was slippery and I lost my footing and stumbled into him. I pushed him over the bank."

"I was already off balance," Lucas muttered. "I slipped in the mud too."

"An accident," Conrad said sharply. "Raining up there," he went on, grunting between the words. "We were all slipping and sliding a lot. Accident."

Mallory came running to them, and took Hugh's place. "Call Dr. Sizemore," he said.

"Don't need a doctor," Lucas mumbled, but even his lips were pale.

Mallory nodded to Hugh. "Call him."

He ran on ahead; when he had finished the call, they were taking Lucas upstairs; Regina lagged behind. Janet, watching the three men go up, said, "You can use my bathroom. A hot shower should make you feel human anyway. Come on."

Her voice was kind and soft and when she put her arm around Regina's shoulders, the younger woman seemed ready to start weeping, but she straightened and even smiled a little. "Thanks. That's what I need." They went up together.

Watching them out of sight, Hugh felt a sudden lurch in his stomach. In his mind there had flashed a brief glimpse of Regina coming down the curved stairs, exactly the way

Culbertson had come down them at their first meeting; she was talking to him, coming down easily, smiling.

Half an hour later he drove back to his house to collect the belongings Lucas and Regina had left there. Lucas was in pain, no doubt the doctor would put him to sleep, and Regina refused to leave him. He gnawed on his lower lip until it was sore. He kept thinking about what Regina had written in her notebook: The game had started and the old man had won round one. Was this round two? If so, it was a second win for the old bastard.

He liked his house and its sparse furnishings. Laura had taken everything she wanted, not leaving him much. He had bought a new stereo, a chrome and leather chair, bookshelves for the living room. The bedroom had only the bed and a chest of drawers. One day he would buy a chair and another lamp, he often thought. Regina and Lucas had left clothes on the bed. Her underwear was on the chest of drawers; his socks were on the floor at the side of the bed. Hugh hesitated at packing up their laundry, then shrugged and tossed it all into an open suitcase and closed it. Let them sort it out. Another, larger suitcase was still in the living room. He took them out to his car, put them in the trunk, and came back in.

He scrambled eggs and watched the evening news on television as he ate, until he realized he was not seeing it. The food was gone. He could not have said what he had been thinking. He put his dishes in the sink, turned off the lights, and headed back to the Culbertson farm. It was fifteen after seven; they would be through with dinner before he got back. Halfway down the block he stopped and returned to his house. He had not picked up her notebook, and he wanted her to continue the journal. He found it stuffed behind a cushion on the sofa. He opened it to the last entry, saw that she had added more, and sat down to read it.

She had added her account of the destruction of the plants. It was practically word for word as she had told it, and in her neat script it was more frightening because the distance was so meticulously maintained.

Hugh closed the notebook, hesitated about taking it with him, then tucked it under his arm and left his house again. The rain had finally started, a light drizzle, the kind that would make the road slick and smear up the windshield.

At the car he opened the suitcase and tossed in the notebook. Let her make of it what she would.

He thought about Janet's analysis of her father's love-hate for women. All the kids had been infected by him to some degree, but children were always shaped by their parents. And Culbertson? What had his mother done to him to make his ambivalence so lethal? And what had happened to her to make her do whatever it had been? It was an infinite regression, he had said once, or more than once. It was his taking-off point, actually. You can keep going backward to find the cause, then its cause, until you got back to the first cause, and then what? Or you could start with now and say *no more*. No matter what they had done, they were not doing it any longer. You could shake off the influence of the past, start over with now, this instant . . .

He had done that when he kicked Laura out, he thought grimly. He had resumed the life of the eligible bachelor without any regrets, or hours spent in recriminations, or trying to justify himself. His mouth tightened. Hogwash! It was all hogwash.

"Right down the line," he muttered, driving too fast. And that was the biggest problem of all: He no longer believed the things he told himself, the things he told his students. He had lost faith in his own lectures, in the years' accumulation of knowledge that had cost him a fortune in money and time. He could not even be certain that whatever Culbertson had done to his children had stopped with his death. Something was happening in that house; they were being affected, and he had no way of knowing what that something was.

Janet's room was decorated in shades of violet with forest-green accents. She had a sewing machine and shelves of fabrics and ribbons, accessories of all sorts.

"I always liked to make things," she said to Regina. "I used to make stuffed animals, toys, things like that. And for a long time I did weavings. I was a better craftsman than artist, as I finally realized. Macramé, my God I've made enough to hang pots from here to Chicago."

Regina sat on the bed; Janet in a rocking chair with an open basket of knitting materials by her side.

"And yet, you left it all here when you moved out," Regina said in wonder.

"I closed the door on the past, something like that anyway. But tell me something about you."

"There isn't much." Regina was sitting where she could see the hallway. The door was open, in case Lucas woke up and called. Every once in a while she thought she heard movement in the hallway, but there was never anything when she looked. "I went to Ohio State," she said. "My family lives in Ohio. And afterward I got a job in New York, and last year I got the job I have now."

Janet laughed. "More abbreviated than that they don't come. What about your family? Brothers? Sisters?"

Regina shook her head. "My mother got polio when I was a few months old, she never recovered from the paralysis, both legs, one arm."

"Good God! How awful!"

"It was all I knew," Regina said quietly. "My father took care of her. He worships her. She's very pretty and kind and clever. I was in the way."

Janet nodded in sympathy. "I know that feeling. We were all in the way in this house. Kids are too disruptive, too anarchic. It's their natural tendency to destroy order."

"Exactly," Regina said. "My parents had each other, neither of them needed me. And I left messes and had to be reminded to clean them up, things like that. Yet, they both love me. I know I love them. It was just better when I got out. They were relieved, I'm sure."

"And you and Lucas? Do you want children?"

"I don't know. Not right away." Why had she lied about that, she wondered. Lucas had made it very plain that he was not in the slightest interested in having children at any time. She looked toward the hallway again, nothing.

"What is it you hear?" Janet asked, reaching for her knitting, looking in the basket.

"Nothing."

"What I keep hearing are the heavy footsteps of a very angry man, coming closer and closer, hitting his leg with something, a rolled-up newspaper, something like that."

Regina stared at her. She shook her head. "Rustling sounds, like the wind blowing the drapes."

Janet straightened without picking up her handiwork. "All different," she said, in a puzzled tone. "Isn't it curious that we all hear such different things."

Now Regina stood up. "I'd better go check on Lucas." Janet made no effort to stop her, and when she had left the room, Regina heard the door close softly. The hallway was very quiet, there were no wind noises.

Hugh was dreaming that he was stretched out in the fields, attenuated to a molecule-thick layer of himself, so that he covered the land, all the land, and the rain was falling gently on him. Below him the land was warm and yielding; he flowed into crevices, up over rocks that were strangely resilient, not at all uncomfortable. He felt himself exchanging ions with the land, then molecules, then whole sections of himself, and that was right, the meld was refreshing, rejuvenating. The rain on his eyelids was cool and pleasant, but suddenly he realized he could no longer locate his eyes; he tried to see outward, see the stars above, a tree, anything. He woke up straining to see; he was sweating and clammy.

For a panicky moment he felt paralyzed; fear jerked him wide awake. His room was dark; no light penetrated the heavy drapes at his windows, the thick carpeting sealed off the lower edge of his door so that no light came in from the hallway. But he had left his door open a crack, and they always left the hall lights on. He groped on the nightstand for his lamp, then withdrew his hand. Instead he got up, felt his way to the bathroom and turned on that light; he opened the door only enough to reach inside to the switch. Very quietly he pulled on his robe; he went to the hall door and opened it slowly, holding the knob to prevent the click of the latch. There was no sound in the house, the hall lights were on, one at each end as usual. The house was very hot. He listened for another minute before going out into the hall. His room was at the end next to the plant room balcony. Then came Janet's room, then Mallory's. Mallory's door was closed although it had been open an inch or so when he passed it on his way to bed. He looked on down the hall. Conrad's room, the door to the front stairs. On the other side was an empty room, Lucas's room, and the master suite. His eyes narrowed. The door to the master suite was slightly ajar.

Slowly he went to it, listening. Damn the house, he thought, such soundproofing wasn't natural. Houses should make some noise of their own, not absorb it all like a sponge. At the door he stopped again. It was dark inside. What he really wanted to do was go back to his bedroom, close the door and lock it, get into bed and bury himself under the covers. He took a deep breath and pushed the door. This was a dressing-sitting room. It was empty. Beyond it light showed in the bedroom. Hugh glanced down the hall toward Mallory's door. Maybe he should get him, have him investigate the light in his father's room. Even as he thought this, he was moving noiselessly toward the bedroom door. It was open several inches, enough to see part of a window, a bed, a table with a shelf of books and a lamp. He pushed the door another inch; a man's figure became visible at a second window. He was looking out at the black night. His head looked very large with hair standing out all around.

"Get the hell out of here!" he said harshly without turning.

Hugh felt hairs rise on his arms, the back of his neck; he was clenching his hands so hard they hurt.

"What in the world are you two doing in here?" Janet asked behind him. He couldn't hide his start. "Sorry. Didn't mean to scare you to death. What's going on?"

The man at the window turned. Conrad, Hugh thought in relief that was so complete he wanted to giggle.

"What are you doing up?" Conrad demanded. "You know you aren't ever to come in here! Get out! Get out!"

Janet clutched Hugh's arm spasmodically as Conrad went on:

"You're hot for him, aren't you, you filthy cunt! You think I haven't seen the way you look at him, the way you follow him around, sit close to him, whisper in his ear. What have you been telling him?"

Janet began to laugh. "Connie, stop it! You can't pull it off, you idiot! You still don't know enough vile words!"

Conrad took a step toward her, stopped and shook his head. He blinked rapidly, as if his vision had blurred. Then he looked around in confusion. "Someone turned the heat up all the way," he said. "I came in here to turn it down again."

Janet was still holding Hugh's arm. Now she let go. "And did you turn it down yet?"

"No. I was just going to."

Conrad went to the wall by the door where he opened a panel and adjusted a thermostat. "He liked to control the heat himself," he said. "Thought we all wasted fuel. Sixty-five, that's where he always kept it."

Hugh watched them without speaking. Inside he was

shaking hard; his stomach hurt, at the same time he felt hungry. Conrad went past him, out into the hallway, leaving the light on in the bedroom. Janet turned it off and she and Hugh left the suite. In the hallway she hesitated.

"It was an act," she said. "He used to pretend he was Father when we were kids. It was a game with him. It gave him a chance to use the foulest language he knew." She did not wait for a response, but hurried down the hall to her room.

October 19

"I READ YOUR paper," Regina said at breakfast the next morning. "There was a lot of it that I couldn't follow, but most of it seemed to make perfect sense. You were kidding, though, weren't you?"

"A little. I think it was a reaction to a lot of nonsense I had come across. There was a continuing story about an exorcism that was the final straw."

Regina played with her scrambled eggs. She buttered an English muffin, added blackberry jam, put it down. She was twenty-six, he knew, but this morning she looked older; she looked mature, he corrected, and very tired. If he asked about dreams, would she tell him? He knew she would not.

"Let me say what I got from your article in a very unscientific way, just to see if I do understand it," she said, and waited for his nod. "Okay. There are axons that are stimulated by something, the axon fires because it has to. At the end of it is a synapse. It takes a certain amount of a chemical substance to cause the synapse to fire. If there isn't enough, it doesn't go off. If there is enough, an exchange of ions follows, potassium and sodium are exchanged . . ."

"That's pretty good. You read it thoroughly."

"Training," she admitted. "I have to read stuff like that now and then. But I got lost after all."

"The axon is stimulated. It releases a quantum of transmitter substance that causes the ion exchange. The charged molecules jump from one synapse to the next where receptor cells bind them, changing that cell's electrical potential, which stimulates the next axon to continue the process. But you're getting at something, aren't you?"

"I think so. It's like a chain reaction, but what stimulates the axon in the first place? What if there isn't any outside stimulation?"

"There's a constant ion exchange going on, as long as you're alive, if only because your body is functioning, and that requires brain activity. You're always getting signals that you're interpreting even when you're not aware of it. In true sensory deprivation experiments, we've found that without external stimulation, the brain continues to function, but because the activity isn't directed in any way we call rational, hallucinations result. But the brain keeps right on working, right up until death."

She was frowning at him in concentration.

"Regina, the brain needs oxygen and glucose. If you take away either, it stops. It oxidizes glucose to develop the energy it needs to reestablish the potassium-sodium balance constantly. It's a machine. A beautiful organic machine. We do understand a hell of a lot about how it functions. We don't have it all, but enough to know that it's a discrete organ, that because it works, we can think. The thought can't come first; it's a product of a working brain. There's no way an outside influence can seize it, control it, and there's no way any thought can exist without the working brain behind it. Thoughts, wishes, images, they are part of a functioning brain; when it dies, they no longer exist."

"I read a manuscript once where the author said that in an experiment a man was able to turn off a switch through thinking. He could generate enough electricity to do that."

"Maybe, in certain very strictly limited circumstances," Hugh said. "That was a controlled test situation in a laboratory, an early biofeedback experiment. And what he was thinking isn't important, only that he was thinking hard. He could have been thinking of artichokes, it wouldn't have mattered."

She rushed on before he could continue. "If we can generate that much electricity with our thoughts, just wanting to do something hard enough, then why couldn't that electricity be stored, the way static electricity is stored?"

Hugh shrugged. "Maybe it could be. Even if that could happen, if enough could be put aside, how would it be used again? That's the rub. There's no mechanism for anything like that. I'm not saying you couldn't save up a store of static electricity, but if you could, how could it be coherent? A jolt of electricity stimulates the brain, no doubt about that, but it doesn't last, and it certainly doesn't generate thoughts that go beyond avoidance of it the next time."

"As for me," Janet said cheerfully, entering the breakfast room, "I'm willing to admit that your mechanistic models work wonders as long as you already know the answers you're looking for. How's Luke?"

"Dr. Sizemore says he's okay. Bruised knee, ligament damage. He's bringing crutches out this morning."

Inwardly Hugh was cursing. Regina had been leading up to something, he felt certain. Five more minutes and she might have told him what.

Hugh left to check in at his office. He drove slowly, drifted past the apple orchard where the pickers were at work; he was thinking of Regina's questions, her intensity, thinking of Janet's acceptance of Conrad's behavior the night before. Why hadn't she been furious, or deeply hurt, or frightened? Her laughter had been almost as shocking as his outburst. Today, he decided, he would stay in town until dinnertime; he was tired of the Culbertson brood, tired of trying to second-guess them all.

He had already missed his morning class, but there was the two o'clock postgrad seminar that Dr. Fields was handling for him this week. He scowled. Help crawled out from under logs, from behind the baseboards, from everywhere, when there was a gold carrot on the stick. No one would make even the most polite inquiry if he failed to show up until next Tuesday. But on Tuesday they would be hot for his body; for word about what the test was, who, if anyone, had passed, when they could start making an inventory . . .

If he didn't do psychology, he thought suddenly, what else could he do? He closed his eyes hard for a moment, then stared ahead at the highway. He envied highway builders, house builders, ship builders. He envied men who planted and reaped, who knew what they were doing, why they were doing it. Pilots, he thought, they knew exactly what they were up to all the time. Laura had said, at the very end, when it was all falling apart, "You've studied enough. You should understand me better than you do. Why do you act as if I'm some kind of alien?"

Because she was. Everyone was. All he could know about them was what they did, never why beyond the most superficial, on-deck reason. If they told him why, he had to be suspicious of their rationale because, he suspected, most people seldom knew why they acted as they did. Janet had gained weight because her father mistreated her. Or because a boy had turned his back on her at some point. Or because her mother had not liked her enough. Because she was afraid of relationships and avoided them by being gross. He shook his head. Janet was not gross, simply overweight.

He drove past the university, straight to his house, eager to be in his own tiny office—solitary confinement, Laura had called it, wrongly. It was a refuge. A chain reaction, Regina had said. Everything triggered by conception? birth? the first traumatic injury? Something. And everything else afterward simply fell into place, as predictable as dominoes, atoms fissioning, axons and synapses firing according to schedule?

Mechanistic models. They played with mechanistic models and pretended they were getting closer to the ultimate secret. What kind of model could he construct that would explain why he had dreamed of being scattered over the earth, being absorbed by it as the gentle rain dissolved him? He could imagine trying to get an answer from Dr. Fields, who would lecture about associational memories and their ability to stimulate sensory memories.

He looked at his wall calendar opposite his desk. Thursday, the nineteenth. He wanted to go over and circle the twenty-fourth with a red felt-tipped pen, but a new circle would be lost in the jumble of circles, crosses, checks, notes. He always started with black, then to call his attention to a particular day he went to green; when that too got lost, he used red. The numbered boxes were a hodgepodge of markings. Above the chaotic mess was Mt. Hood, glaciated, remote, untouchable, unchangeable, winter and summer always the same gleaning white slopes, the same exterior that concealed so well the scars of its fiery birth. He liked volcanic mountains. They lied with such grace and beauty.

He brought himself back to his desk, back to his notes, and cursed briefly because his Dictaphone was in his campus office. He started to scribble notes about the last two days. Gradually he forgot his frustration as he tried to

recall every word, every gesture each of them had made.
Someday, he had thought earlier that week, all this would
be the genesis of a new paper, maybe even a book, but he
had forgotten that and was interested simply in getting it
all down, almost as if he knew that within the bulk of the
material he was accumulating, there was a fragment that
would provide the key to the whole, and he dared not
overlook it.

Mallory and Conrad had brought Lucas down to the television room where he was stretched out on the leather
couch. Dr. Sizemore had given him muscle relaxants to
keep him quiet and off his leg. It would need rest for a
few days and gradually he could begin to get around again.
Lucas dozed, and then as the medicine wore off, he became irritable until it was time for his next pill. On a
coffee table pulled next to the couch Conrad had placed
a bucket of rocks that Lucas had collected in eastern
Oregon.

"There's a lapidary outfit down in the basement," Conrad said, looking through the rocks. "We all worked at it
from time to time. Look at this one. Nice, isn't it? Picture
jasper."

It was a flat rock with one side cut and polished to a
high sheen. The background color was buff, there was a
band of pale blue, and behind that deep blue in the form
of mountain peaks. A single streak of yellow looked like
moonlight through clouds. Regina caught her breath as she
studied it. It was a miniature painted by a master. Lucas
glanced at the rocks and then looked away scowling.

"Why'd he keep all that junk around?"

"He always liked to cut and polish them, too, you
know," Conrad said, picking up a blue agate.

Lucas pushed at the table and struggled to a sitting
position.

"Can I get you something?" Regina asked, pulling the
table out of the way.

"No. I'm going to the bathroom."

When Conrad made a motion as if to help him up, he
jerked back out of reach. "I can manage."

He walked out awkwardly on the crutches. Regina
waited until he was out of sight and then sat down heavily
on the couch.

"Hey," Conrad said softly. "It isn't your fault that he's being a devil."

"He thinks I pushed him over that ledge. I guess I did."

"Regina, we both know it was an accident, and so does he. It's this house. God knows what memories he's reliving, and now he's confined to a couch on top of all the rest of it. And I bet that damn medicine is too much of a depressant for him to tolerate."

She looked at him gratefully. "I bet that's it! He never takes any medicine, not even aspirin. I'll call Dr. Sizemore and ask him if it might be too strong." She looked at the phone on the desk, then shook her head. "I'll use the one in the library. Be right back."

She hurried to the library and placed the call, only to learn that Dr. Sizemore was with a patient at the hospital. He would return her call in an hour or two, his receptionist said. She hung up and started to leave the room, then paused. This was where the old man had spent most of his time. That soft-looking chair with a good lamp and a roomy table by its side. She could imagine him sitting there, reading about possession, the occult, gradually coming to believe in it, brooding about his children, about leaving this beautiful estate to one of them when he knew none of them could ever love it the way he had done. She could sense his pain at thinking how they might change it, destroy an image here, a vista there, let the roses go wild . . . You had to be attuned to it, be aware every day of what needed doing, when to prune, when to fertilize, when to replace a tired plant. You had to anticipate the sweep of colors before they came into being or you wouldn't know when something was off, when something was faded, or too bright. First it existed in the head, then on the land. There would be drawings somewhere, she thought, and found herself walking toward cabinets under the windows. Drawings, plans, schedules. Someone had to follow the schedules he had worked out over the years; someone had to study the detailed ground plans drawn painstakingly on graph paper, every plant clearly positioned and labeled.

"Regina! What are you doing in here?"

Lucas stood in the doorway balanced on his crutches.

For a moment she felt only confusion, then she remembered. "I wanted to make a phone call." Without a glance at the cabinets she walked to the doorway where he moved aside.

"Who were you calling? Who do you even know in these parts? Was it someone in New York? Someone you're missing? Is that it?"

She stared at him in bewilderment and passed him without answering.

"Don't you walk away from my questions like that! Who were you calling? Viola! Come back here!"

She felt as if she had plunged into the pool again, this time over her head in icy water that squeezed the air out of her. She was running, through the hall to the stairs, up to their room, to the bathroom where she slammed the door and locked it and pressed her forehead against it. "What's happening to us?" she moaned. "My God, what's happening to us?"

And she thought of what she had wanted to talk about to Hugh Froelich. Pockets of static electricity. Pockets of hatred and madness waiting for them to stumble into, waiting to take them over, make them behave in crazy ways, say crazy things. If Lucas had not interrupted her, she would have found the drawings, plans, everything. She didn't know what she would have done with them, but she had been meant to find them. And Lucas, he had not intended to say what he had said. He had stumbled into another pocket of insanity and had acted, unable to stop. When he came into the bedroom and called her name, she opened the door and held out her arms blindly and they clung to each other helplessly, both of them weeping.

Hugh stopped working for lunch, then went back to his notebooks. He was almost finished when Conrad called.

"Know when you're planning to come back?" he asked.

"Might not today. I might stay in town and get very drunk instead." He was immensely pleased with the impromptu plan.

"My God! What an idea! Mind if I join you?" Conrad laughed, then said, "Seriously. I'll buy."

"You might not be in shape to get back tonight."

"I'll talk you into coming back with me. You won't get as drunk as I will. You're not the type."

They arranged to meet at six, have dinner at Cleo's Clam House, drop off the car Lucas had rented, and eventually head back to the farm.

"Do you know exactly what he meant by sleeping in the house each night?" Conrad asked before hanging up. "Full eight hours, starting at midnight? A couple of hours starting at dawn? What?"

"No idea," Hugh said. "Ask Bill Strohm."

"I will. I'd better find out before, don't you think?"

After Hugh finished his notes, he went downtown to buy gin, vermouth, and onions. Gibsons, he had decided. They'd get smashed on Gibsons. Corvallis was a town where the shopkeepers called their customers by their first names, asked about the job, the kids, the fruit or nut trees, whatever was important. That day they asked Hugh about the Culbertson kids.

"Heard funny things happen in that place. Luke get hurt?" Jimmy, at the liquor store, studied Hugh with frank curiosity.

"He slipped in the mud by the river," Hugh said. "Nothing more mysterious than a little fall on the rocks."

"Yeah? Funny about that place, all the accidents that keep happening." He rang up the sale. "You see anything funny up there?"

"Nope. It's just dull."

"Yeah, I guess. You take care, Hugh. It's a funny place out there."

Funny, Hugh thought, that summed it up. Conrad arrived on time, and they had two Gibsons before they left the house. Conrad talked about his work, his concern with feeding the hungry world, the need to control unwanted vegetation so that food could be grown instead. During dinner he drank three mugs of draft beer while Hugh sipped sparingly at a glass of wine; he had found that he didn't want to get drunk after all, not if he had to drive back to the farm. Conrad talked about his two exes, and Hugh talked a bit less about his one.

"You know why we do it, really?" Conrad asked later.

"Do what?"

"Anything. Everything we do. You work with heads. I work with poisons. You know why?"

"Tell me."

"Because we can. Simple as that. I learned how in school, and now what else is there for me? I mix my chemicals and test the stuff on a plant. You screw around with a brain. The old man fucked over the land. Women screw you over coming and going. Same thing. You do what you can do."

They went to one of the student hangouts where the

music was too loud and the voices were louder. There was
Foos Ball and pool and dancing, the air was sweet with
dope. Conrad didn't like that place and they drifted on to
another, then another.

"The old man could make a rock grow," Conrad said
later. "Truth. Tongue depressors, they'd grow for him.
Used to send him our house magazine, full of pictures and
stuff about killing plants, my name all over it. Wished I
could see his face the first time, every time. Spend my life
looking for more and better ways to kill plants. What
would a shrink make of that?"

He was glassy-eyed, tilting dangerously when he moved,
yet he kept talking coherently, without any blurring of his
speech. "Saw him whip a girl once," he said much later
with his eyes closed. "Truth. Took a quirt and beat her
with it. Naked back, belly, everywhere but the face, so
nothing would show. Said if I moved, he'd kill her. Believed him. Watched. Pretty little thing."

He stood up, weaving back and forth. "Witching hour.
Bill said reasonable hour. Two is reasonable hour. Three is
very unreasonable, but two is okay."

"What happened to Janet's mother?"

"He snapped her neck like you snap a dead bloom off a
flower. Snippety snap. Probably didn't mean to. Mad as
hell for weeks because she bought something or other. A
car. She bought a car for herself, so she could come and
go, and she only went. Snap. She fell backward down the
stairs, soft like, just a little noise like leaves falling off the
trees, flutter, flutter, sigh."

"Why wouldn't they believe both of you? Two of you as
witnesses. Why didn't they believe you?"

"He was in Salem and she drove by and tooted the horn
of her new little car. He left the party to follow her home,
ran up the stairs after her, yelling about her being a no-
good whore out running around all night. He snapped her
neck and then he ran out, back to the party and no one
even knew he had left. They said he never left. And Mallory was a liar, and I was under Mallory's influence, and
Janet was left without a mother." He had been leaning
forward, then back, and from side to side. He sat down
abruptly and put his face down on his arms. "I was good
and drunk and you made me sober again. Son of a bitch."

A waiter had been trying to get in close; each time Hugh

had waved him away. He beckoned him now. "Double bourbon."

Conrad drank it straight down without opening his eyes.

"Let's go home," Hugh said, and guided him out of the tavern to the car, got him inside, where he passed out immediately. Hugh drove carefully. He was drunk enough to end up in the tank if he ran a red light, or was caught speeding, or anything else. Not drunk enough, he thought bitterly, to not give a damn.

Mallory met them at the door and helped get Conrad up to his room. "I'll tuck him in," Mallory said. "Strohm's downstairs, asked if you'd come down for a couple of minutes. If you don't want to, I'll tell him to make it tomorrow."

Hugh shrugged. "I'll go down. Is there coffee?"

"Yep. In the television room." Conrad was sagging between them. Hugh helped lower him to the bed, then started out. Behind him he could hear Mallory murmur, "You really tied one on, Connie. Come on, first the shoes."

In the hallway, Hugh looked at the end door to the balcony and thought, almost triumphantly, it wasn't working. The old bastard had been wrong about them; they were as close as ever, maybe closer.

Strohm was scowling when Hugh entered the room and went to the table for coffee. "I'm surprised you can walk."

Hugh ignored him until he had his coffee and was seated by the fireplace where a log was glowing. The room felt close and too warm.

"Look, Froelich, I want to make something clear. I don't like that goddam will any more than anyone else does, but we have it. I don't know what constitutes a night in the house. The old man overlooked that part. Don't you make it tougher for all of us, okay? They want to wander out and stay, that's their business, but you don't have to cooperate."

Hugh didn't look at him. "Go to hell."

"I don't intend to have that will contested on a technicality," Strohm said furiously. "You'll be given a statement to sign and have notarized testifying to your own knowledge concerning who was here and who wasn't. If they miss even one night, they're disqualified. Period. And if it's contested on that basis, and you're involved, you'll have something to answer for to your own school administration. Don't kid yourself about that. What if you'd been arrested for driving under the influence? He'd be out, and it would be your fault." He got up and went to the door. "After two, for God's sake!"

A few minutes later Hugh heard a car leave the driveway, squeal at the turn, fade into silence on the lava road. He didn't move. He wondered if Strohm had argued with Conrad about going out to get drunk, if he had brought up the possibility of disqualification. Conrad had not mentioned it. He got more coffee and, as he was adjusting himself in the chair, it occurred to him that he should not have heard the car leave. Not in this soundproof house.

His stomach churned and for a second he thought he was going to be sick. Slowly he put his cup down on the end table, watching his hand which was not very steady. Even more slowly, he stood up and walked from the television room down to the main hall. A cold draft chilled him; the front door was standing wide open. He went to it, past the living room, past the end of the stairs. Strohm? Not in a million years, he thought clearly, would Bill Strohm leave a house door standing open. He stood in the doorway looking, but there was nothing to be seen: the wide porch with more hanging baskets of plants, the dark shadows of dogwood trees beyond the porch.

Someone had gone out, he thought. Or had someone come in? He felt the hairs on his arms prickle, and whirled around almost expecting to see someone standing close to him. Make him stop, he thought; go out and make him stop. Go out. He slammed the door and leaned heavily on it, then groped for the lock to make certain it was set. Every night Mallory or Conrad went through the house checking the windows, setting the locks; every morning the doors were all unlocked to be left that way all day. The old man had hated to have to fish out a key to get inside his own house, Mallory had said, and he had refused to give his children keys. He wanted to know exactly when they came in at night. Hugh pushed himself away from the door and took a deep breath. The urge to go out there had passed as completely and as suddenly as it had overcome him. His stomach was hurting dully, as if he had been hit, and his head was aching with the throb of a hangover. Damn Bill Strohm, he thought, damn his eyes, trying to turn him into a baby sitter, an informer. He hoped the son of a bitch crashed into the bridge, went down the bank, over and over. He had a quick vision of him lying in the swift water that turned pink and rushed away, but it wasn't Bill Strohm. A woman with long brown hair . . .

Laura! He pressed his hands over his eyes so hard everything turned red. He was shaking. Laura! Something had happened to Laura! He hurried back to the television room and snatched up the phone, dialed without having to think of the number; when she answered after many rings, he looked at the telephone blankly and hung up. He sat down staring at the log in the fireplace. It was barely smoldering now. He sat without thinking, without seeing; when the sky turned pale, he went to his room, fell into bed, and slept deeply.

October 20

It was ten when Hugh woke up. He had a headache, and was twitchy; there was a foul taste in his mouth. He stayed under the shower for a long time. Should have stoned out, kept the hell away from booze, but he always thought that after a night like last night.

He went downstairs and headed for the kitchen. Anita would be gone. She came in early, made breakfast if anyone wanted it, straightened up, vacuumed, and then left until twelve. She was in and out all day. He didn't go down the hallway to the television room, from where he could hear raised voices. They had left the door open; most of the doors were open more often than closed these days. He shuddered and moved faster. No arguments this morning, no lectures.

Mallory found him at the kitchen table a few minutes later. "We want you," he said without preamble. "I'm going to make more coffee and bring it."

With a sigh Hugh went to the television room where all the others were already assembled. Conrad's eyes were bloodshot, his hands trembled, but he grinned at Hugh. "Partner," he said cheerfully. "Want an aspirin or six?"

"Yeah."

Conrad motioned toward the table where there was a bottle of aspirins. Hugh shook out a couple, poured coffee, and sat down. No one looked much better than Conrad, actually. Lucas was still too pale, the cut on his cheek was shockingly red; Regina looked like a prisoner in the dock. Janet was doing her needlepoint furiously. Hugh had never seen anyone make such fast stitches.

"Have you been outside yet?" Janet asked, not looking up.

"No, why?"

"Someone cut down all the dahlias and most of the roses," she said. "It's an unholy mess. Anita wanted to call the police and Mallory wouldn't let her. She may quit."

"They think I did it," Regina said tightly. She sat apart from the others.

"No one thinks you did it," Lucas said.

Regina didn't look at him. She kept her gaze on Hugh. "I want to hear Mallory say that. Yesterday I got some shears from the potting shed to cut flowers to bring in. They all acted as if I had defiled a sanctuary or something. *He* never let anyone cut a flower, it seems. They think I went out in the night and cut them out of spite or something."

"For God's sake, be reasonable!" Lucas snapped. "Mallory asked a simple question. Where did you leave the shears? That wasn't an accusation."

"You know damn well where I put them! You all saw me leave them in the kitchen! I felt like a thief caught stealing the crown jewels!" Her voice broke, became shrill.

Janet kept looking at the work in her hands. Now she murmured, "And that's the problem. We all did see the shears on the floor by the kitchen door. And this morning they were outside, smeared with rose stems. Someone took them out again."

Hugh got up and went outside. He followed one of the bark paths to the rose beds. Roses were strewn everywhere, some of the bushes cut off near the ground, others butchered randomly. He circled the area and looked at the dahlias. Here the destruction looked even more total. Not a dahlia had escaped. The flowers had been cut and trampled, jumped on apparently, crushed into a filthy mess. How long had it taken? An hour, more than an hour?

He returned to the house. Mallory was pouring coffee into a cup; he took it to Regina.

"I'm sorry it sounded like an accusation, Ginny. No, I don't think you did it. You and the professor are the only two who don't have a lifetime of murderous hatred and anger stored up, ready to pour out at a word. I'm sorry."

Her face had been stony, marbleized; it crumpled and became the face of a little girl grievously hurt. She blinked hard as Mallory patted her shoulder, and then Lucas was at her side holding her as she wept.

"But it does have to stop, now doesn't it?" Conrad drawled. He waved toward the coffee. "Mallory, would you mind. I don't think I can move my head."

Mallory refilled his cup, took one for himself and sat down. Regina pulled away from Lucas and blew her nose. "Sorry," she mumbled.

"It does have to stop," Mallory said heavily. "If Anita had called the police before I got down, we'd be in a real mess. It would get out, you know. Everything does."

"Villagers with torches, carrying pitchforks, barking dogs, the works," Conrad said lazily. His eyes were not sleepy. He was very aware, very alert.

"Did any of you see or hear anything?" Mallory asked. His voice had a harsh, desperate huskiness. No one answered.

"It could have happened any time after dark," Conrad said. "How can we be sure it wasn't Anita herself, or Carlos? Either of them might have had cause to hate the old man and his precious flowers."

Mallory shook his head. "Carlos loved him. He shared his feeling for this farm, everything on it. And Anita? No way. If you had seen her this morning, you wouldn't even suggest her. Besides, the shears were there when I saw her out and locked up."

"Then why did you ask Regina where she left them?" Lucas demanded.

"I hoped she'd say she remembered them and took them back to the potting shed," he said.

Hugh kept thinking of the open front door, feeling the urge, the need really, to go out there and stop someone. His stomachache was coming back. It had been like that, he remembered, when he had had swimming lessons—a terrible fear and a stomachache, day after day. Maybe he was getting an ulcer. Regina was right, he was too tense, too wound up all the time. He put his cup down. He would start drinking milk, no more booze, no more coffee. He said, "Last night after Strohm left, I found the front door wide open. I closed it."

"How long after he left?" Conrad asked.

"A few minutes—five, ten. Mallory was probably still getting you undressed."

"I woke up fully clothed," Conrad muttered and he closed his eyes.

"I couldn't do anything with him," Mallory said. "I left him and went to bed." He rubbed his hand over his eyes. "Wait a minute, there was something." He frowned at the floor, then went on in a low voice. "I was untying his shoe and I stopped and just sat there with him for a while. I was remembering how it had been when he was small, I think. Finally I started to pull off the shoe, and I was madder than hell without knowing why. It scared me to be that mad. That's when I went to my room."

"Are you sure you went to your room?" Janet asked. "Are you sure you didn't go out there and do that first, get it out of your system?"

Mallory shook his head. "No. I'm not sure. God help me, I can't be sure." He took a deep breath. "God help us all if I did it," he said softly. "Because if I did, I don't have any memory of it, and that scares the hell out of me."

There was a long silence which Regina finally broke. "At least the dahlia roots can be dug up and saved for next year. And the roses would have been pruned anyway."

Hugh was watching her as she spoke; he saw her become even paler. "What is it? What happened?"

"I don't know anything about dahlias. I never saw them growing before," she whispered. "Is that what you do, dig them up and keep the tubers for next year?"

Mallory nodded. "You read it somewhere."

"Bet not," Conrad said. "Come on, Mallory, we've all said and done things this week that we had no business saying or doing. I know I have."

"What?"

"Quoted you a price for fir, and I know damn well I haven't followed the market. No reasons for me to." No one else spoke and Conrad laughed deep in his throat. "Luke, no little confession to make?"

Lucas shook his head; he was watching Conrad fixedly.

"Funny. Could have sworn you pulled a tantrum over nothing and even called Ginny Viola. Didn't he?" He turned to Regina, whose pallor had spread alarmingly.

That was what she had been leading up to in the breakfast room, Hugh realized. Pockets of static electricity, someone else's electrical charge left hanging in the air for various people to blunder into and be transformed by momentarily. And wouldn't that be neat? Sooner or later they would use up the charges and it would all be over.

"This isn't getting at the problem of vandalism during the night," Mallory said. "Knock it off, Connie."

Lucas had not denied it, and Regina had not said a word, Hugh noted for later consideration. He wanted pictures of the various wives, he decided. Wasn't Viola Lucas's mother? He thought so.

"I propose that we take turns staying up at night," Mallory said. "Since we can't bring in anyone, it'll have to be us."

"I was probably here in this room when the flowers were getting mowed down," Hugh said. "I didn't hear a thing."

"You were drunk," Mallory said.

"Not a bad idea," Conrad said. "If it's my shift and the pictures get hacked to pieces, I'll be the first to blame. Right?"

"We'd expect whoever is up to keep a lookout, to stay awake, to check through the house at regular intervals. And yes, if anything happens during your shift, it would look bad. For any of us, it would look bad."

"Luke can't," Conrad drawled. "What about you, Professor?"

"He doesn't have to," Mallory said. "This is a family problem."

"I'd like to," Hugh said, "if you have no objections."

"This is my mother, Sally," Janet said later in the library, handing him a photograph. The woman was beautiful, with black hair that hung down over both shoulders in soft waves; her eyes were dark blue with heavy lashes. She had a model's face, lovely proportions. Janet handed him another one of her mother, this time riding a horse. Slim, vibrant looking, laughing, she was even prettier than in the first photograph.

"Here's Conrad's and Mallory's mother, Winona." She too had dark hair, but she was not as beautiful as Janet's mother. Winona was tall and long-legged, wide-shouldered.

"She was pregnant and the baby wasn't his," Janet said matter-of-factly. "That's why they fought. My grandmother told me."

"How did she know?"

"Arithmetic. Winona was three months pregnant and he

had been in Washington for six months, working for the rationing board after Pearl Harbor."

She was flipping pages of the album, looking at the loose pictures, and now she handed him another one. "Viola," she said, "Lucas's mother."

His stomach spasmed like an attack of appendicitis. It hadn't been Laura that he had glimpsed in the water. It had been her. Viola. Long brown hair, like Laura's, but there the resemblance ended. Laura was handsome all the time, sometimes she was pretty, and there had been times when he had known she was the most beautiful woman he had ever seen. But Viola had started beautiful and could never have been not beautiful. Well-spaced brown eyes, soft brown hair, straight nose, wide, full mouth. She was what people meant when they talked about classic beauty.

"What's wrong?" Janet asked, shaking his arm. "You look like you've been sandbagged."

"Nothing. It's nothing."

She took the photograph from his fingers and replaced it in the album. "Nothing. Right. Whatever you say."

"I'm going out for some air. Thanks, Janet. Thanks."

"Sure," she said dryly. "And remember it's all coincidence, Professor. There is no mechanism for anything else."

He felt sandbagged, he thought, standing by the outside door, taking in deep breaths. Around the side of the house Mallory and Carlos were cleaning up the mess in the rose garden. Carlos had already dug up the dahlias. Today the air was almost cold; there was a brisk northeast wind coming down from the mountains, frost weather. He stared dully at the fields across the road; it never had occurred to him before to wonder if there would be frost or not, if the weather would change. There had been no reason for him to care. He started to walk.

Today Conrad had taken Lucas and Regina out for a ride, just to get them out of the house. Regina was convinced that there were those mysterious pockets where crazy things happened to you. And Janet was still going through the books on possession, searching for something, symptoms maybe, signs to watch for to indicate it was happening. Hugh felt a helpless fury inside himself, like a dull hot pain growing in his gut. That bastard, he muttered, that goddam bastard . . .

He walked to the river and found a flat rock to sit on.

Light flashed on a trout, then it vanished again. He picked up a stone and threw it in, hoping to scare the fish out. For a long time he threw stones into the water as hard as he could. It was ten feet down from the bank here, probably about that at the bridge; the water was only a few feet deep, then very shallow as it foamed over rocks.

Conrad was right, he admitted. They had all done and said things they had no business doing and saying. Role-playing? Janet said Conrad had liked to pretend to be his father when they were young. Weren't they all doing that, pretending, acting out the game the way they believed it had to be acted out? It had been Laura's face he had seen. There was no way for it not to have been. But he didn't want her dead. He had never wanted her dead. Liar, he heard in his mind. Liar, liar, liar. He threw a stone hard, watched the splash, then another and another. He no longer knew if he had seen Viola's face or his former wife's face, and it didn't matter. He had seen it the way he could conjure up an intact memory of his childhood, the house he had lived in, his dog, his parents. A clear, intact, visual memory. The synapses for those visual memories offered less resistance than synapses to new, never-before-seen fantasies. The template was there, forever waiting with its message intact; this way, this way. Either he had remembered that brief glimpse or hallucinated it; he didn't like the choices.

He heard steps behind him and turned to see Mallory approaching.

"He used to come down here to fish," Mallory said, stopping several feet away. "That's his rock."

Hugh jumped almost reflexively. "That's a hell of a thing to say after this morning."

"Yeah. I know. About standing guard, what are we going to do if we catch anyone in the act? I didn't want to bring it up at the house before. We should have something in mind."

As they walked back Hugh thought about the .38 he had locked up in his file. Laura had insisted on having a gun in the house. If he caught Mallory in the act, what then? Shoot him?

"We should have a good loud whistle," he said. "Wake up the house."

Mallory nodded doubtfully. "We'll have to do something

about keeping the doors propped open. Mine seems to want to close after I get to sleep."

"Mine too. I'll fix it somehow. Anyone touches it from now on, I'll know."

Anita had left. Mallory and Conrad had checked the doors together, now they were all in the television room where Janet, Lucas, and Regina were playing Scrabble.

"What the hell is a graupel?" Lucas demanded.

"Want to challenge me?" Regina asked, laughing.

"Goddam it! Okay, I challenge you."

"It's a kind of snow. Granular, I think."

Next they would be playing charades, or twenty questions, Hugh thought. It was a lot like summer camp during a rainy spell. Irritable, getting on each other's nerves, restless, they were all showing signs of cabin fever.

"As soon as Anita comes in the morning, I'm going to take off," Mallory said suddenly. "I'm going home for the day, be back before ten probably."

The others had messages for his wife and children. Janet even looked envious for a few moments; she was the only one who had no way to break the monotony, Hugh thought. If she went home, what would she go home to?

"You'll get me up at four-thirty?" Mallory reminded Hugh.

"You bet." Each of them would take a two-and-a-half-hour shift, starting with Conrad. The whistle was on the desk; Mallory had dug it out from his room, a bit of his childhood that had hung in place for thirty-five years.

They all drifted off to bed soon after Mallory went up. Hugh spent several minutes fixing his door. He leaned a glass against the top of the doorframe, balanced precariously on the top of the door itself. If it opened or closed, the glass would fall. Under it he put a cookie sheet he had borrowed from the kitchen. He tied a string around the knob and attached the other end to the lamp by his bedside. He hoped no one would look beyond the first booby trap. He settled down to read, but didn't get to the bottom of the first page before his eyes began to blur. He felt that he had just turned off his light and pulled up the covers when he heard his name being called.

Downstairs, every interior door was standing open, lights were on in every room. He nodded in approval. There was fresh coffee in the kitchen and a plate of sandwiches under a glass cake cover on the table. Beside that was the whistle on a shoestring. He slipped it over his head and then sat down and ate two sandwiches, drank two cups of coffee and afterward made the rounds to check windows, to make certain the outside doors were all locked. At the sunroom he hesitated briefly, cursed himself, and entered. In this room there were sliding glass doors to the covered deck, another door on the far wall. He hurried past the bed, examined the windows and doors and left again as fast as he could.

When he finished, it was only a few minutes after three. He went to the library and stood looking at the shelves of books. Art history? He pulled one down. It had been used; some of the pages had been dog-eared, then straightened again, leaving the crease line. Philosophy. History. Lots of history. Religion. Many religions. A Torah, several Bibles, the Koran, the Upanishads. Some of these books looked especially old, much used. Probably he had bought many of them in used book stores; this room had not been outfitted by an interior decorator. These books had been picked out, bought because he wanted to read them, shelved to be read again. There was a shelf of nut books, he noticed, everything from UFOs to the Bermuda Triangle, Charles Fort's works, dowsing, and ESP. What had he not been interested in? Very little fiction. Shelves of books on the occult. What had he got rid of in order to shelve the new things?

There was a deep leather chair with a lamp. Slowly he went to it and turned on the lamp; he switched off the overhead light. He sat down in the leather chair and put his feet on a matching ottoman, reached out to the end table with one hand, to his shirt pocket with the other. Where the hell was his book?

Hugh jumped up abruptly. "No! Get out!" The sound of his voice jolted him. He ran from the room, back to the kitchen where he drank a glass of water, splashed more on his face, shivering as it ran down his neck. Anita put it away, he thought, and his stomach cramped so hard that he vomited without warning.

After a few minutes he cleaned up his mess and opened the kitchen door to air out the room. He felt numb and very cold, his mind was strangely blank, as if he was suppressing every thought as it formed. It was almost four.

He stayed in the kitchen for the next half hour, and

only when it was time to go upstairs to rouse Mallory did he close the door and lock it again. The kitchen was frigid; he had meant to make a fresh pot of coffee, and had forgotten. He forced himself to put it on to perk before he went up and whispered Mallory's name outside his room, not touching the door for fear of setting off a booby trap. As soon as Mallory answered, he staggered on to his own room, closed his door, and fell across his bed in instant sleep.

October 21

HE WOKE UP feeling dull and achy. Saturday. Sunday to go, then the second round of EEGs on Monday morning, and Tuesday the reading of the will and the famous test. He groaned at the thought of getting through three more days.

When he entered the breakfast room Janet was crying shrilly, "Just go on and leave me alone! Don't keep trying to arrange my life!"

"He wasn't trying—" Lucas started.

"Stay out of this! He's always tried to tell me what to do, ever since I can remember. But no more, Connie. Just get out and leave me alone."

"Righto," Conrad said. "Suits me."

"Wait a minute," Regina said, looking from Janet to Conrad. "I don't want to go off and leave her alone."

"The professor will be here," Conrad said indifferently.

Regina turned to Janet. "Will you wait at your house until we come back, let us pick you up there?"

Janet glared at her for a moment, then sighed. "I'll wait for you. Don't rush. Go on and have dinner. There are a lot of things I should get done at home."

"We're going to the coast," Conrad said to Hugh. "And Janet's going shopping with Anita and then home. What are your plans for the day?"

Janet snorted and threw up her hands in disgust.

"I just want to know if we should give him a key."

"I'll go home too," Hugh said. "I have things to do."

"Okay. I'll tell Anita to take off the rest of the day. She deserves it. Ready, kids?"

"Sorry about all that," Janet said as soon as the others were gone.

"Good idea to get out of here for a few hours, forget the whole thing."

"Like forgetting a toothache."

Hugh drove to his office to collect his mail; he brought his notes up to date, and then stared at the wall clock wondering what he would do all afternoon. There were things he had been neglecting, but he would continue to neglect them a little longer. Students' work seemed very unimportant. There was also a memo to call Dr. Fields, which he regarded sourly. Not now, he thought. Fields couldn't do anything but ask questions; he had no answers, no one had answers. Also, if he talked to Fields, he would be ordered to stay the hell away from that house. He dropped the memo back on his desk, gathered the mail, and went to the door, then returned to his desk and got the Dictaphone disk. He would transcribe it himself someday. He didn't want the department secretary to listen to the things he had said.

He shopped for dinner and ducked questions. The whole town must be buzzing, he thought as he hurried to his car. When he entered his house the phone was ringing; it was Ben Cowper, one of his colleagues at school. He wanted to know what was happening.

"Talk to you about it later, okay? I'm in a bit of a rush right now." Ben protested until Hugh hung up. A few minutes later the ring started again. He didn't answer. It rang twice more in the next fifteen minutes, until finally he pulled the plug. He did his few household chores, ate lunch, and wondered again about the rest of the day. Moodily he lay on his bed and tried to avoid thinking about the farm, about his probable ulcer, focusing instead on the coming Monday and the new EEGs. Hardly anyone was using them in research anymore; like so many discoveries that seem to be breakthroughs initially, this one had found its niche and had become simply another tool, available if needed. It had passed from the experimenters to the practitioners.

Suddenly he sat up. Sizemore wouldn't have given Culbertson the EEG. Sizemore was a G.P.; he would have sent him to a neurologist. Yet the old man had distinctly said he had given it. Hugh frowned, recalling that evening over four years ago. Culbertson had said they thought he might have had a stroke, that was the reason for the test. Slowly he got up and went to his office. He found Sizemore's number, dialed it; he got an answering service. He sat unmoving until Sizemore called back in half an hour, peevish at being interrupted on Saturday afternoon.

"Four years ago did Culbertson nearly die from a heart attack?"

"That's your emergency? For God's sake!"

"Just tell me. Did he?"

"Yes. Clinically he did die. Greta massaged his heart until the ambulance got there and a paramedic took over."

"Did you order the EEG for him?"

Sizemore cursed and said no.

Hugh thanked him and hung up. Why had he lied about it? That explained the elevator chair to the balcony, but why had he lied? And that meant that he had had no medical reason for the EEG. Had he ordered it made in response to Hugh's article? He held his temples hard; the headache he had awakened with had diminished and now was rushing back with reinforcements.

He had spent three hours with the old man. They had talked about politics briefly, the weather even more briefly—when Culbertson realized how little Hugh knew about meteorology, he had changed the subject. He had been knowledgeable though, not only about meteorology, but about geology and physics as well as Hugh's own subject, psychology. And he must have had access to the journals, or he never would have come across Hugh's paper in the first place. Where were his science books and magazines? Hugh suspected they had been cleared off the library shelves to make room for occult nonsense.

He went over his notes one more time, listened to his own halting dictation that left out a lot because it sounded foolish, and then he read through his copy of Regina's journal. He wondered if she had resumed writing in it, and with the thought came an intense desire to see anything new she had added.

At the last minute Janet had handed him her key to the house; in case, she had said, he got back first there was no point in his waiting in the car until someone else showed up. He felt in his pocket; when he brought the key out, he knew he was going back. He would take his steak and cook it there.

He noticed with approval that they had rearranged the furniture, had pushed the twin beds together. Regina, he suspected, was enthusiastic in bed, she had that look about her. If pressed, he would not have been able to say exactly what he meant by that. A twinkly look, was how he defined it. Lucas looked like a man who had no need to wander afield at all. Also, Lucas had the look of a man with a latent streak of jealousy. If Regina became successful, began hobnobbing with famous authors, went to conferences, that latency could become an active, mean force in their lives, he felt certain, unless Lucas himself was equally successful. Or, he thought clearly, unless the Lucas he saw here was not the same as the New York Lucas.

He found the notebook in a drawer along with other school books. Purloined letter, and it would have worked if he hadn't already pried. He took the notebook to the window to sit where he could see the driveway; the shame he felt at snooping was overwhelmed by his curiosity.

There was actually very little that he hadn't already learned. She had come to like the entire family, and had written observations about them all: Janet had been afraid she might be like her mother and had reacted by gaining weight and becoming as unattractive to men as she could. Also she had not learned to drive and didn't own a car. Another one: Mallory was frightening sometimes because he was so ethical. Hugh grinned and nodded. But, Regina had added, he didn't try to impose his standards on anyone else, and in a strange way that made him very vulnerable. Again Hugh nodded; she was perceptive. He remembered what Janet had said about the old man—he had his own moral code. He found a bit about Conrad: "He is so full of self-hatred that I just want to take his hand and tell him he's okay, really okay. I don't think he would understand . . ."

Hugh saw again that dark lanky figure standing at the window in his father's bedroom, heard the terrible things he had said to Janet. He recalled Conrad saying that he and Hugh did what they could do: he in chemical warfare of a sort, and Hugh screwing around with heads.

He kept reading, suddenly his heart thumped erratically.

He read: "There isn't any warning, no little tendrils of fear creeping through your mind, no feeling of an invading presence. There's just another way of perceiving, not your way. And you know he's there, or something's there. If we stay here, I will lose my mind, I know.

"Lucas and I promised each other that if either of us wakes up at night, we'll wake the other one before we get up, even if only to go to the bathroom. We're leaving the bathroom light on and the door open. I woke up suddenly, the way I did the other time, all at once wide awake as if it were morning. I sat up and looked at Lucas sleeping. I reached out and touched his hair and I thought, 'Stop hating me. For God's sake don't hate me. You're all I have left.' And I knew. I screamed a little I think because Lucas woke up and I was crying and saying, go away, just go away."

Hugh turned the page; there was only one paragraph left.

"We won't make love in this house, not with him here watching all the time, able to get inside our heads. Lucas is terrified that he might hurt me and, God help me, so am I."

Which *he*, Hugh wondered: Lucas or his father.

Bluebeard's sons, he thought with a shudder. Slowly he got up and replaced the notebook. They were all in a state of heightened suggestibility. Not hypnotized, but so suggestible that any stimulus, even self-induced, made them react. And their reactions were not their usual ones, but what they believed his would have been.

He pressed the theory further as he walked downstairs. If Regina did anything to anger Lucas right now, he would not sulk or pout, or do any of his Lucas things; he would fly into a rage, insult her, possibly try to hurt her. Not consciously play-acting, of course.

He had walked down the hallway to the front door. Now he paused and turned to look back toward the unfinished living room. Lights were on in there, people were talking. Someone was talking to him at the door; he paid no attention, but strode past him to the living room. At the door he stopped and stared in horror. The unfinished floor, walls without the interior paneling, the curved stairs without a banister, all lighted with floodlamps. On the floor, Sally lay contorted, her head twisted to one side, one leg doubled under her.

"No," he cried. "No!"

At the front door Hugh sank to the floor on his knees. His stomach was twisted in knots, doubling him over. He rolled once or twice as the spasms receded and finally left. He felt sore and didn't try to get up yet. Appendicitis? Cancer? Something bad, he thought. See Sizemore? He shook his head. Not Sizemore. His own doctor. Monday he would see Owens. He pulled himself up by the side of the door and sat with his back against the wall for several more minutes. Another hallucination? Something was attacking his gut and his head all at once. Cancer that had already metastasized?

His mouth felt like cotton, the way it had once as he came out of an anesthetic. Holding on to the wall behind him he got to his feet carefully, afraid another attack would start with any sudden movement. His stomach felt tender. He walked slowly, keeping one hand on the wall; when he came to the living room, he paused to look inside. The room was awash with late afternoon sun. That was where she had lain, there the sheriff had stood, and behind him his deputy, and over there the sleeping bags . . . He would recognize any of the men if he saw them again. But they were thirty years older now, he thought, and he began to hurry to the kitchen for water.

He drank one glassful without pausing, then refilled his glass and sipped from it. There was a notepad on the wall by the sink. He pulled it down and sat at the table to write a description of the woman he had seen. Green shiny dress with a full skirt, gold slippers, an ankle chain, bright-red fingernails, rings—an emerald set with a diamond, a gold band—earrings, also diamonds, garish makeup. She had looked like a high-priced whore, he thought, and knew that was right. Sally had been a lovely high-priced whore.

Abruptly he stood up and tore off the paper he had written on and shredded it, threw it into the trash can. He stalked to the library to find the album that Janet had shown him. It was put away in a cabinet under the windows, along with two others. There was no picture of Sally in a green dress or with that particular jewelry. But he must have seen it somewhere. He drew out a second album and began to go through it page by page. This one had snapshots and clippings, and in it he found an account of Sally's death, listed as an unsolved murder. Culbertson had spent the evening at a formal banquet given for Samuel Petryk, one of the board members of the university. The two Culbertson boys had seen someone on the balcony with Sally. There had been an argument and a struggle and she had fallen. The assailant had run downstairs and out before either of the boys could identify him. The motive had not been robbery, the article continued, and listed the items of jewelry that the dead woman had been wearing. Hugh closed the album and jerked at the explosive noise it made.

He had read it before, maybe even four years ago, and had forgotten. Or someone had told him when he had been asking questions. In his head he heard a dry, rattling laughter.

The trip to the coast was not a success. Lucas sat in the back seat of Conrad's car with his leg stretched out before him, but he kept shifting as if he could not get comfortable. Regina was glad when they finally reached the coast highway. Another time she would love to make the drive again, slower—stopping now and then to wander in the rain forest of the coastal range, where ferns and mosses grew atop each other in abandon—but today she had been too aware of the silence that no one seemed able to break, too aware of the discomfort Lucas could not hide. They had no small talk, she thought regretfully, none of them did. She ticked off the many people she knew who could have kept a conversation going all the way and wished she had even a little of that ability to keep talking without thinking about it.

"And there is the calm Pacific," Conrad said then.

Her first view of the ocean confirmed his description, an expanse of the bluest sea she could have imagined. They rounded a curve and she also saw the shoreline and gasped. Here the waves broke in a frenzy amongst half submerged boulders, the water boiled, shot upward in jets, roared. Conrad drove slowly until he found a lookout, where he stopped and they sat in the car without speaking, taking in the scene far below. There was a stretch of wide beach, the endless parade of waves that from here looked small, and then, farther, water crashing against boulders.

"We can get closer," Conrad said, driving again. For the next hour he stopped and started along the road that dipped close to the water, then climbed precipitously, hugging cliffs, corkscrewing, before plunging back to sea level.

"You should take her down to the tide pools, show her some starfish," Lucas said. His cheeks were flushed from the wind blowing through the car. Regina kept opening her window and closing it again; she wanted nothing between her and the sea, but realized she was chilling everyone. She closed her window once more.

"I know a place," Conrad said. "I think I remember." He drove on without stopping again until they reached a pullout that had picnic tables and parking spaces. No one else was there.

"You getting out?" Conrad asked Lucas, who shook his head. "We won't be more than a few minutes."

They scrambled down the cliff to a stretch of exposed basaltic flows that the sea had carved and recarved as if deliberately sculpting homes for the shore creatures. Regina ran from one pool to another marveling at the gaudy starfish, the countless crabs, anemones of pink, purple, green . . .

A wave broke around her feet and Conrad called, "Time to go up. The tide's turning."

Her ears were tingling from the cold, her fingers had turned scarlet from dipping her hands into the pools, feeling, lifting the starfish, putting them back. Even her toes ached with cold. Her feet were soaked. She followed Conrad up the cliff, holding on with her hands at the steepest places, and when they reached the top, she turned to look one more time. Already the incoming waves were flooding the pools that had been exposed only minutes before. As she swung around to go to the car, she caught a motion from the corner of her eye, something pale, and she realized it was Lucas standing at the edge of the cliff staring out at the sea. He was not moving; the wind was blowing his open Windbreaker, ballooning it in the back.

She dared not call out to him, dared not startle him. Slowly she walked toward him, feeling the cold within her now.

The wind was full in her face, making her eyes smart and tear. She drew close enough to see his jaw muscle clenched in a hard ridge, to see his hands white on his crutches.

"Lucas," she said faintly. She stopped, not quite within reaching distance, afraid to move closer to him. "Lucas?"

He turned and looked at her, his face as composed as that of a dead man.

"Let's go," she said, still speaking softly. "It's getting awfully cold."

He continued to regard her without expression. She saw his chest rise as he breathed in deeply; he nodded and backed away from the edge of the cliff until he had enough space to swing one crutch around, make the turn, and start back awkwardly over the rough ground. Neither spoke again.

Now she could see Conrad midway between them and the car. He looked haggard and old. He knew, she thought. She could not meet his gaze. They all got inside the car and he turned on the heater.

"We'll go to Mo's," he said. "Good hot chowder, that's what we need." It sounded as if he were reading lines from a book.

Hugh had meant to put it off until the next day, instead he found himself confronting Mallory that night. "Why did you swear it was your father who killed Sally? You were old enough to know what you were doing."

"What the devil are you talking about?"

Conrad was in front of the television reading, while an inane show played itself out. Janet was busy with her needlework, and Lucas and Regina were looking at rocks. They both had been subdued since returning home. All motion in the room stopped with Hugh's question.

"I mean it was impossible for him to have seen her in town and follow her home that night. He was at a formal dinner where he was one of the speakers. A banquet, for Christ's sake! Speakers' table. You can't just duck out for a couple of hours and not be missed."

"They'd lie for him."

"No. You know those men wouldn't lie about a thing like that."

"We saw him!"

"How? No lights were installed yet. All you could have seen were figures, blurs against the windows. You had been sleeping when you heard the noise. You didn't have time to make out anyone."

"I saw him," Mallory said grimly.

"You saw something," Hugh pressed. He felt as if every muscle in his body were stretched out so much that he would twang if anyone touched him. "That's how vision works. We see something and we compare it with past experiences and expectations and identify it. You believed it was your father, and you 'saw' him. How long have you known you were mistaken?"

Mallory jumped up and shoved his chair back hard. "What are you suggesting?"

"You've known for a long time, haven't you? How long?"

Mallory started to move toward him with his fists clenched. Hugh wondered if the others would sit still and watch him be beaten to death, wondered if he could outrun Mallory.

With one easy motion Conrad was on his feet; he stepped to Mallory's side, took his arm. "Go on to bed. You've had a long, tough day and you're due to stand guard at four-thirty, remember. No more smashed pots or uprooted flowers."

Mallory kept looking at Hugh almost blankly. "Sure," he said. "Good night."

Conrad drew him to the door and watched him a moment. "Why did you do that?" he asked without animosity, as if Hugh had just impaled a butterfly.

"To clear the air a little. If he didn't kill Sally, maybe he didn't kill anyone. Maybe there's a lot of misplaced hatred floating around this house."

Janet heaved herself up, glaring at Hugh. "Maybe yes, maybe no. We'll never know for sure. But even if you could prove that he didn't, it doesn't change anything. He wanted them all dead. He wanted me dead. And now he wants to destroy everyone in this house. That's the kind of man you're trying to defend."

"Wanting people dead is not the same as killing them," Hugh said angrily. "Don't be childish."

"I think you'd better leave," Janet snapped.

"No. I was invited to stay."

"Have you looked in a mirror today, or yesterday? Do you have any idea how you've changed since you got here? You're the one he's getting to, and you don't even know it." She stared at him another moment before she went out.

"How did you know about the lights?" Conrad asked, watching Hugh with narrowed eyes. He looked anything but sleepy.

"I read the stories and today it occurred to me that the way you and Mallory told it just couldn't have been right."

"How did you know we'd been sleeping?"

"I assumed you had been. The sleeping bags were by the fireplace."

Conrad returned to his chair and sat down heavily. "You didn't read that in the papers, Professor. It was left out deliberately. They always leave out some details so they can sort out false confessions from the real thing if it comes along. No word about sleeping bags."

Hugh moistened his lips. "You must have said something about them."

"Nope. Didn't. We agreed not to mention them."

"I guessed then. What else would you have been doing down there at that time?"

Conrad didn't answer. Regina and Lucas must have signaled each other, Hugh thought with irritation; they stood up together and walked from the room, almost whispering good nights.

He could still remember the sleeping bags: one red plaid, the other dark green, side by side in front of the mammoth fireplace. The boys had not been in the room. Conrad watched the television; the sound had been turned down all the way and Hugh could not remember when he had done that. A newscast had come on.

"It's scary, isn't it?" Conrad said finally. "Maybe for you and me more than for the others, actually. Because we both know damn well it can't happen, and we both know damn well that something impossible is happening."

Hugh wanted to deny it, to explain again. He remained silent.

"Scary," Conrad repeated softly. "You'd better go on to bed. I'll call you at two." He turned up the sound on the TV and a commercial for dog food blasted the quiet.

This time he could not go to sleep. He lay rigidly, listening for a sound in the preternaturally still house. From his open window he could hear a light wind sigh in the screen from time to time, nothing more. Mallory's door had been closed and Hugh began to wish he had closed his also; the light from the hall was bothering him, but he did not get up to remove the booby traps and close the door.

He wondered what Janet had meant by asking if he had looked at himself. People always did. Brushing teeth, combing hair, women putting on makeup, men shaving. He could not remember looking at his own face in days, and that meant there was nothing unusual to see, or he certainly would have noticed, especially now when he suspected that he had something seriously wrong with his stomach.

He tossed, remembering the way they had regarded him, as if he finally had shown his stiletto-sharp teeth. Why had he done it tonight instead of waiting? He had no better answer than the one he had given earlier: to clear the air. Instead he had polluted the air, possibly past cleansing. Now they would all be watching him, waiting for him to pounce again, gathering tighter together against him as the common enemy. He had seen it before, the child-molester parent defended by the battered child against the common enemy—the social worker, or the judge, or the psychologist.

He drifted into sleep only minutes before Conrad called his name, and he was dopey and sluggish when he went down. He doused his face with cold water, but he was so tired that he was afraid that if he sat in a comfortable chair, he would fall asleep again. He took a book to the breakfast room where he perched on the edge of one of the straight chairs with coffee before him.

It was the wrong book, he thought, and got up to get the right one. He went to the library, to the shelf of occult books, shook his head, then looked at the books someone had left on a long table.

Janet, he thought. Goddam that fat slob, never could put anything back where she found it. The book he was looking for was on the table—*The Ultimate Experience.* He took it back to the breakfast room and sat down again, started to read.

Without noticing it he had picked up his coffee cup; he felt wetness on his fingers and glanced up; his hand was shaking hard. The awful fear seized his stomach; he dropped the book in horror. With a wild cry he threw the cup through the window.

"No! Get out!" he screamed.

This time the painful attack was shorter than the last and not as severe. When it ended, he wiped his forehead with the back of his hand. He was sweating. He stood up shakily and went to inspect the window. A cold draft was coming through, chilling the sweat, making him shiver. He found a paper bag and cut it open, rummaged through drawers until he found Scotch tape, and sealed off the broken window. He printed on the paper in large letters: SORRY. I WAS TRYING TO HIT A MOUSE WITH THE BROOM. There had been a flashlight in the drawer with the tape; he got it out and took another bag outside to pick up the pieces of broken cup. He hoped Anita Mantessa would accept his story about a mouse. Poor woman, mice on top of everything else; no wonder she wanted to quit. He would too if he could.

If he could, he thought with a bitter laugh. If he could. He reached the mess outside the window and began to sort out the broken cup from the shards of window glass. He could always say he tried to hit it with a cup; he kept picking up bits of pottery.

He knew now why someone had destroyed the plant room and the gardens. It was a method of resisting. The shock of action, of violent action, seemed enough to make it stop, whatever it was. He sympathized with the one who had been driven to such extremes, and while sympathizing, he felt afraid of that unidentified person. Someone was headed for banana-land for sure, and that one was violent and could become dangerous. He had finished picking up what pieces he could find. It was very cold outside, there would be frost. Stop it! He didn't give a damn if there was frost, snow, hail, whatever. He went back in and deposited the rolled-up bag in the trash can. He made himself a drink and wandered over the lower floor carrying it. Only when it was nearly time to get Mallory up did he remember the book he had dropped, and he retrieved it. Tomorrow, he promised himself, he would read it tomorrow. He took it to his room when he went to bed.

This time he closed his door and turned the lock. He did not care if they slashed and hacked to bits everything in the place. He was too jumpy to go to sleep right away, although he was so tired every movement was an effort. Finally he looked over the book he had picked up in the library. He had read several other books and a number of papers on the ultimate experience, death, and he tended to discount them all. The researchers made a big deal of the differences between the people they interviewed: rich people, poor, educated, uneducated, religious and irreligious

. . . What they overlooked was the fact that they all had in common that even more ultimate experience, birth. That was the first, the most traumatic crisis anyone experienced, and no one arrived equipped with language to sort out the memory of it. Experience without language with which to codify and express it remained sensory, to be restimulated only by another experience, equally sensory, equally traumatic: death.

He read the book with growing impatience, muttering now and then. "Idiot! Walking into the arms of Jesus! Shit!"

He was skimming rapidly, not finding what he sought, angry with the nonsense he was reading. Couldn't any of those fools see? Couldn't they grasp what they had been offered? Suddenly Hugh shuddered. Again! He threw the book across the room and waited for the spasm in his stomach. This time it did not come.

October 22

"IN YOUR PAPER," Regina said the next morning, "you talk about how memories are formed and stored. RNA is manufactured and acts as a template to give you the memory of what you saw?"

Hugh nodded. "That's about what we think."

"What if you have memories of things that never happened?" She glanced at Lucas who was looking stonily out one of the windows. The brown paper was still taped in place.

"Hallucinations aren't real, but if you have one, you'll remember it," Hugh said. "And fantasies, daydreams, dreams themselves. If the thought goes through the works, it leaves its own memory trace."

"And things you didn't hallucinate or fantasize or dream?"

"You did, or you wouldn't have the memory," he said simply, believing it. This morning with the sun brilliant outside, pancakes and sausages on the table inside, he believed precisely what he said. "We stop at the skin," he said, and went on more sharply than he had intended, "and we stop completely with death. There's absolutely no evidence to support anything else. Believing something else is a form of wish fulfillment or fear mongering." His memory served up a taunt from his childhood: "Liar, liar, your pants are on fire!"

Regina was shaking her head. She had not eaten much. No wonder she was thin, stress turned off her appetite. Janet obviously reacted exactly the opposite. Suddenly

Hugh felt a great sadness for Janet, who had refused herself the solace of food this past week.

Lucas hauled himself to his feet, grasped his crutches. "Come on. I told you it was crazy talk. I wanted you to go home, remember? I didn't want you to stay here this week." He hobbled from the room.

Regina looked as if she might weep. She took a deep breath. "He's being hurt," she said quietly. "I don't know how or why, but whatever it is, I think it's going to kill him."

"Regina, look at me. No one has been threatened this week. No one. Whatever we're all doing, we're doing to ourselves. Please accept that."

She looked at her plate.

"Regina, who paid for Lucas to go to school? Who paid for his therapy?"

"His father. Not directly, through a trust or something. Why?"

"And Conrad's Ph.D.? And Mallory's down payment on his ranch? Years of schooling for Janet? He paid for them all, didn't he?"

"I don't know. I guess so. What are you leading to? What difference does that make?"

"I'm not sure. But it does make a difference. I just can't believe that after all those years of taking care of them one way or another he would turn on them now. Think about it. There's no influence in this house, no haunts, no ghosts, only memories, and if they're threatened by their own memories, there's nothing you can do. The memories are all you have, finally. You are your memories."

"That's fine," she whispered. "I accept that. I just don't want to be his memories too. And neither does Lucas." She got up. "I'd better go find him."

"Regina, wait a minute. You think Lucas is in danger. What kind of danger?"

She looked at the door before she answered in a low voice, "That day up in the woods, I think he intended to jump. I convinced myself that I was wrong, that it was my fault for grabbing at him the way I did. But he had a look on his face that I'd never seen before. And yesterday at the coast I saw that look again. We were on a cliff. You know the coast, how it is?"

He nodded. Cliffs, vertical rock walls, now and then an easy descent, but not often.

"Did Conrad see either incident?"

"Yesterday he did. I haven't talked about it with Lucas. I'm afraid to."

"He may need help, Regina. There are people who have a deadly fascination with heights and sometimes they do jump, not because they are even especially suicidal, no more than most people anyway. Something else seems to come over them. You should talk to him about it, urge him to get help."

She looked at him steadily. "He's never shown anything like this before. Not in the slightest. It's his father."

"Up in the woods? At the beach?"

"Distance doesn't matter."

"Christ! There isn't any way . . ."

"Never mind," she said gently. "I'll watch him for the next few days. We'll make it."

And who will watch Regina? he thought, remembering her kneeling among the broken flowerpots. He took his dishes to the kitchen where Anita Mantessa said Conrad and Mallory would like him to join them in the library. Now the old heave-ho, he thought, and could think of no good reason to refuse if they asked him to leave the house.

"Would you close the door?" Conrad said, as Hugh entered. Neither of them was sitting in the deep leather chair. They had chosen the bow window instead, a third chair had been drawn in close.

"I wanted to tell you," Mallory said heavily. He looked ancient; his eyes were sunken and the pouches under them were almost black. "That night we went camping, Conrad and I. It started to rain, our tent was leaking, and we got pretty damn miserable, so we came back and made a fire in the fireplace. We planned to get up at dawn and come back in through the back door so he would never know anything about it. And we fell asleep. The fight woke us up, and so help me God, I thought I saw him up there with her. I didn't lie about it. I thought that was what I saw. And I whispered it to Conrad and he saw it too. It was like you said: dark, we'd been sound asleep, it was a shock, too quick to think about, all that. Then he was gone. And I still thought it."

"The point is," Conrad said in his slow, quiet voice, "it could have been. He could have done it. We both knew that. He hated her; they fought all the time. Sally was a bitch and he was a devil. Well paired. I never doubted that he did it until last night."

Past history, Hugh wanted to tell them, leave it alone. But they couldn't leave it alone. It was too alive, too immediate, forcing them to act in strange ways. It was a threat to everyone in the house to leave this particular past alone.

"Later, when Luke came to me and I learned that his mother, Viola, was dead, an accident, I wanted to kill *him*," Mallory went on, looking out the window. "I got a gun and came over here to kill him. We stood looking at each other in the living room and he said to just do it. Everything he touched died, and he was tired of it. Just do it. And I couldn't. I ran out and drove back to Pendleton as fast as I could go. I never saw him again until last week." He stopped and ran his hand over his face, then went on with the same expressionless voice. "Driving home, I knew. I kept seeing that other night, shapes up on the balcony, a man. Just a man, not him. I knew, and I was glad I hadn't realized it before. I swore I'd never tell him, let him die thinking his children believed he killed each wife in turn. I wanted to punish him. But, God help me, I didn't tell Luke either. How much influence that had when he finally remembered his mother's death, I'll never know."

No one spoke for minutes. Conrad broke the silence. "A while ago Mallory and I went up to the balcony and looked out at the bridge. From up there you can't see the abutment. Bushes in the way."

Hugh nodded. "Lucas reported what he believed happened. He didn't see it?"

"I don't know," Conrad said. "He believes what he said. So did I."

Conrad stood up. "Air-clearing time's about over. We wanted you to know. No point in your staying on now. Whatever's going on here doesn't really concern you."

"If you order me out, or even ask me to leave, I'll go. Otherwise, I dealt myself in with that stupid paper I wrote. I'll see it through."

Mallory remained silent, keeping his face toward the window; Conrad motioned toward the door with his head. "You're in," he said. "Two more nights. You don't run the course this far and then stumble and fall down, now, do you?"

Hugh left them in the library and wandered outside to walk in the sunshine. Sometimes that's exactly what you did. With your hand inches away from the goal, you faltered and grasped air. Maybe he would call Laura today, ask if she had received his check. And maybe not, he mocked himself. It had been a surprise when she said she was leaving; he had never suspected it would come to that. Shoemaker's barefoot children, he thought. He had not seen her or listened to her for years, according to her, and he could admit that probably that was right. Not really listened to her, not really looked at her. Nine years was enough for most marriages to endure, he had told himself; after that you're simply in a rut that's comfortable and dull and safe. He could think all those things, rationalize by the hour, and yet he wanted to call her and talk to her more than anything else he could think of, even though he knew he would end up more frustrated than he was now. He kicked at a clump of grass and walked faster.

He looked back at the house. It was very beautiful with the dark evergreens surrounding it as if on guard duty, contrasting with the flame of the dogwoods, the more subdued glow of the golden maples. Peter, Peter, Pumpkin-Eater, had a wife and couldn't keep her. Put her in a pumpkin shell . . . and she died. Or went to California.

He had stopped moving; his hands were clenched hard. He opened his fingers slowly. Whose wife went to California? Not Culbertson's. Laura, he thought with effort, Laura had headed south, leaving him flat. In his head he was seeing the photograph of Winona, Culbertson's long-legged first wife.

He was walking again, seeing the three women, Culbertson's three lovely wives. He had liked them young and pretty and he had not been able to keep a single one of them. Lost his wives, lost his kids. But he could grow sticks and stones. Poor John Daniel, child of nature who never learned how to cope with people, who never learned how to nurture a human relationship. Poor little rich bastard.

Up until his first death, Hugh thought sardonically, the old devil had been willing to share his wealth with his children even if it was all done through intermediaries, the trust funds, trust officers, whatever. After that death, he had decided to punish them. Make them sweat a week.

Try to break the bond that held them all fast to each other. Had it actually infuriated him so much to learn that he was mortal after all? Had he really believed he could possess one of them, continue inside someone else's head and body? More than likely he had simply gone completely bonkers; maybe that was why he had had the EEG made, fear that he had gone crazy.

Hugh sat down with his back against a tree, the sun on his face, his legs stretched out before him. He had climbed higher than he had realized. He had a view of the house, the yard, gardens, the road, bridge, the railroad . . . He could see the bushes that obscured the abutment. Maybe they had not been there then. They had though: The bridge was ugly; he would have screened it from the house. As Conrad had said, it didn't really matter. Except to Lucas. And by now he probably knew one way or the other. Haunted, as Mallory was, by guilt? He should have told Mallory and Conrad to let go, to stop using the past to explain themselves. He almost laughed. What junk he fed into anyone who would listen: a bite of this, a dollop of that, a sip of something else. And come out whole and healthy and nonneurotic like good little girls and boys. Existentialism is all well and good, he said to himself, if there's nothing in the past goading you into actions you'd rather not commit.

That was the rub. They were doing things they didn't want to do, or one of them was, at least. And Lucas might well be looking down from high places and yearning for release. Two more goddam days, he said to himself. Two fucking days. He was very much afraid it was too long. Not the days, he corrected himself; they were able to handle the days. It was the awful nights.

Hugh reentered the house through the kitchen, where Anita Mantessa was preparing lunch.

"What was Mr. Culbertson like to work for?" he asked.

She looked at him without surprise. "Good. Fair. He said what he wanted done and expected it to be done. There was never any problem."

He knew this was hopeless; she was not going to tell him anything. She went on slicing zucchini. "Did you move a book from the table by the leather chair in the library?" He felt his stomach tighten as he said the words.

"Yes. It's in his bedroom, on the shelf of the nightstand."

She did not look up, and after a moment he said thanks and left. He had not wanted to ask; he had been determined not to ask, and now, having asked, he swore to himself that he would not go up there and find the book. When he went up a few minutes later, he had no opportunity to enter the master bedroom: Janet and Conrad were talking outside her door. He nodded and went to his room.

At lunch Janet said, "I've been thinking that grapes should do well on that slope where you were today, Hugh. Southwest exposure, nice ground . . ." She put her spoon down carefully and clamped her lips tightly together.

"Making plans?" Lucas asked. "You think you'll be the one, is that it? After the way he treated you, you think he'd give you a penny's worth of shit?"

"Lucas!" Regina cried. "Stop it!"

"Why? Aren't you looking for excuses to huddle with the shrink? Maybe he'll pat you on the shoulder, feel you up a little, make you get all warm and pink and shivery. You'd like that, wouldn't you!"

"Luke, shut your goddam filthy mouth," Conrad said softly, clipping each word.

"Oh my God," Mallory groaned. "This is how every meal in this house used to be. It's like stepping back into my childhood."

Janet was very pale. "Please, please," she whispered. "If you feel him, you can resist. You don't have to say his words." She left the table, left the dining room. No one asked how she had known where Hugh had been that morning.

It was late in the afternoon before Hugh found a chance to go into the master bedroom. Regina and Lucas were holed up in their room. Hugh had suggested, through Conrad, that they go back to his house for the afternoon. Lucas had refused. Now they had all scattered, the house felt empty. Hugh stood inside the room waiting for his eyes to adjust to the dim light. The drapes were closed and were very nearly opaque. He went through the sitting room into the bedroom, to the nightstand. On the shelf were the Joseph Campbell books on mythology, the entire set. He groaned. Whatever you wanted you could find in them, he knew. He turned on the lamp, withdrew the first book and leafed through it rapidly, looking for annotations, or loose paper, anything. He was looking for a book the old man had written in, and this wasn't it. He did the same with each of them and knew he was defeated. He breathed a sigh of relief.

Even if he had found a diary or ledger or a book with his writing in it, what then? He knew that then he would have felt exactly like Chicken Little; his sky would have fallen. He reached for the lamp switch, took one last look at the volumes that were like old friends—he had an identical set at home—and then stiffened. When he glimpsed that shelf the night Conrad played Let's Pretend, it had been full. Now there was an empty space. He tried rearranging the books, spreading them out, and all the time he knew that wasn't how they had been. A book was missing.

Finally he gave up the pointless shuffle and he turned off the lamp; the room was plunged into perfumed darkness. A woman gasped in the adjoining room, then screamed shrilly. "Yes, I brought him here! In your bed! What did you expect?"

Hugh had no memory of moving, but he was standing in the doorway of the dressing room; the room was dark and empty. He blinked and lights were on, and Winona was screaming into his face, a smear of blood on her lip. "You put me in this jail and left me! What did you expect me to do?" He slapped her again, harder, and her screams became louder. "You'll never know whose child it is! You'll look at it and wonder and you'll never know! Every time I touch it and kiss it, it'll be him!" He hit her again and she fell across a chair. Then he saw a child watching in terror. A thin child hardly more than an infant, too horrified and too frightened to whimper.

The child backed away, reached the door, and fled.

"You can't do this to me," Winona sobbed. "I won't stay!"

"You're getting out all right! Tonight. I'll have no bastards in my house. You're not fit to touch Connie or Mallory, or even be in the same house with them!"

Hugh was standing in the hallway leaning against the wall. It had been something bad, he thought; he could not remember what it had been, or why he was leaning against the wall, or where he had been going. After a while he straightened and began to walk toward the end room. He was halfway there when it hit him and he doubled over in agony and fell to his knees. Someone called his name, and hands were helping him, getting him to his bed. The pain was subsiding by then; he pushed weakly at the hands that were trying to undress him. It was Conrad, behind him was Janet.

"I'm okay," he muttered. "It's over."

"You're sick," Janet said. "What is it? It looked like an attack of appendicitis. Are you sure it's over now?"

He nodded. "Yeah. It's okay."

Conrad held his wrist a minute, then felt his forehead. "No fever, I'm sure. Can you sit up?"

"In a second," Hugh said. He was afraid to try yet. The soreness in his stomach was worse than before, worse than anything he had ever felt. He took several more deep breaths and sat up, swung his legs over the side of the bed.

"Talk about gut reaction," Conrad said lightly. "This is a classic. Our troops are falling by the wayside."

Hugh didn't look at him. "I'll be okay for my stint."

"No way. It was ridiculous to split up one little night among three big men. When I was in the army, it was nothing to have to stand guard twelve hours straight, in freezing rain, snow, whatever the good Lord served up. This is a picnic."

Hugh was grateful for his light patter. It filled in those few extra seconds he needed before he tried to stand. Janet went to the door, gave him one more intent look.

"Thanks," Hugh said.

She nodded and left. Hugh looked at Conrad. "You too. Thanks."

"Nada, nada. What we all need is a good drink. I wonder if Janet couldn't reward her own good behavior with just one little snort." He frowned and shrugged. "But I won't be the one to tempt her. You coming down?"

"After I wash up a little, change my shirt."

"Right." He looked at Hugh curiously. "It'd be easier on the old system, Professor, to smash up the furniture or something. You know? No one here would give a damn, if you just own up to it. It's the mysteries that are getting to us all."

Hugh grinned at him. "I'll keep that in mind."

"Carry an inkwell at all times," Conrad said. "See you over the booze."

Dinner was silent and no one showed much appetite. Anita had made apple pie; she served it, and brought a slice of melon for Janet, who groaned and said, "It's true that all good things are sinful, carcinogenic, or fattening." It was the first time that she had referred to her diet. Regina managed a faint smile for her effort. No one else seemed aware that she had spoken.

"The plan's changed for tonight," Conrad said. "Since Hugh's sick, it'll just be Mallory and me—"

"I'll take a shift," Lucas interrupted.

"There's no need," Conrad said. "I can easily stay up until three, do it all the time, matter of fact. And Mallory gets up early every day of his life."

"I'll take the professor's slot," Lucas insisted. His voice grew firmer, louder. "I have a stake in this, too, you know. In spite of what some people might think." He shot a dark glance at Janet, who seemed unperturbed.

Hugh was content to be excluded. It didn't matter if anyone stayed up or not, except to interfere with more vandalism, and he didn't care how much any of them destroyed. The real threat could be carried out in daylight, morning, afternoon, any time. The real threat was not a few broken pots or mutilated flowers. The real threat . . . He stopped because he no longer had any assurance that he knew what the real threat was.

The bickering went on until Mallory abruptly left the dining room. Conrad shrugged and gave in. Regina and Lucas would stay up until two, playing Scrabble or chess or something, and then awaken him. Anyone could blow a whistle, Regina had said angrily at one point. You don't need two good legs, and you don't need to be six feet tall. And, she added, she would not stay upstairs alone while Lucas was downstairs at night.

Janet turned to Hugh. "Exactly what do you expect to get out of all this? I assume he paid you something for the work you did, the EEGs, and the ones you'll do again. Is that all?"

"I'm not sure. He paid me five thousand, and I admit I can use the money. He suggested that I might want to write another paper, or even a book, afterward. I don't think so."

"I suppose he thought you would be able to remain objective. Wrong, of course. At least you're not emotionally involved, not like we are."

"Not emotionally, or financially either. I've had all I had coming. Look at this from an outsider's point of view. You all have cause to hate him, and for whatever his reasons, he apparently hated all of you. His entire life was one of losing people—wives and kids. Maybe it warped him. He had a heart attack four years ago and nearly died." They really had not known, he thought, watching their reactions. Surprise, doubt, confusion, more guilt? He could not read their expressions well enough to know what passed through their minds. He continued, "It's true. You can ask Sizemore. Anyway, when he recovered, he changed his will and arranged this whole encounter group. Think of the ingredients he managed to include: a fortune in real estate, isolation for an extended period, strict rules about who can be here and who can't, even a piece of technology to make it look scientific—the EEG before and after. And he made certain his interest in possession was obvious. If the word had never come up, you couldn't have failed to notice the nutty books in the library. I think you all underestimate his intelligence and his grasp of psychology. He knew exactly what he was doing. And I would bet the five thousand he paid me that he knew what would happen almost down to the last detail."

Luacs looked both angry and disbelieving. "He wasn't that smart."

"Yes, he was. I talked with him on two separate occasions, remember, and I was not a kid scared to death of him, or hating him for anything and everything. We talked about mass psychology and he understood the subject thoroughly. He had read a lot over the years. He understood about expectations, about heightened suggestibility, about fear and guilt and the power of associative memory. He knew almost as much about stimulus-response mechanisms as any practicing psychologist. He knew damn well that the response may be delayed twenty years, or thirty years, but that eventually it will happen. He was counting on that."

"Hear, hear," Conrad said; his voice lacked conviction.

"I think we're having a freshman lecture," Janet said, getting up from the table. "Also, I think the professor is planning to write a paper after all, that he's been thinking quite a bit about what will go in it. It could present an interesting legal problem."

Hugh didn't bother to deny it. He had not been thinking those things at all. It surprised him that he had been able to present such a convincing case without preparation. Push my button, he thought disgustedly, and watch me dance! S-R lives.

Hugh sat at his window looking at the dark countryside wondering why no one had asked the obvious question: Why? Why had Culbertson changed following his massive heart attack? Why had he spent months, maybe even four years, preparing this grotesque experiment?

It was raining and the night air was warmer now that the weather was coming from the Pacific instead of the mountains. He liked the Pacific fronts that came with a regularity that was almost moon-phase dependable.

In his room, Mallory was staring into darkness, going over and over scenes from his childhood, that night in the unfinished living room, hating himself, hating his dead father more.

And Conrad was awake, full of self-hatred because he had let the old man whip Janet until she fell unconscious. He had let it happen, paralyzed by fear of the threat of her death, more terrified that he would be beaten, that he would be killed, and suddenly convinced that she had it coming to her, that it had been her own fault. And with that thought had come the real terror that he was exactly like his father.

Janet lay thinking about the apple pie at dinner, almost smug that she had resisted although she had wanted it so much it had been a physical ache. She thought about her mother's beautiful gold sandals with glass-needle heels and ankle straps. She had wanted shoes just like them, she had wanted those shoes so much that she had sneaked into her mother's room frequently just to slip them on and teeter about, pretending she was grown up with lovers coming to call. She could remember nothing else about her mother, only that she had been beautiful and had worn gold sandals, and of course that she must never be like her, act like her, look like her, or she would be evil and he would kill her.

In the library Lucas and Regina watched a late movie; the sound was too loud, but neither wanted to turn it down. Without it the silence was unbearable. In the silence you could hear them, Lucas was thinking; they were around corners, in the next room, behind you. Screaming, cursing . . . And Regina was thinking: When he was talking after dinner, I believed him, all of it. I don't believe in ghosts. What he said sounded right. I should keep repeating key phrases—stimulus and response, stimulus and response, stimulus and response . . .

Hugh jerked away from the chair in which he had been sitting. He was very cold. He had fallen asleep after all, sitting up with the draft from the open window on him. Dreaming of them, all of them by turn. He had been dreaming, he repeated. Now he was wide awake. He glanced at his watch and was dismayed to find that he had been in his room less than half an hour; it was only eleven-forty now. And he was wide awake.

He tried to read and could not understand the words, which seemed foreign. He could not concentrate on anything long enough to make a note. He began to walk back and forth from the window to the door, thinking about that hallucination in the master suite. He had actually hit her, many times. He could remember how it had felt when his hand struck flesh, how satisfying it had felt. The scene played on the surface of his mind where he could rerun it over and over, and suddenly he found that he was seeing Laura's face, not the other woman's. It was Laura that he was beating up, relishing beating her up, wanting to keep hitting her again and again, and not just with his open hand. She deserved it, he thought, just like the others, all of them.

He had been pacing faster and faster; abruptly he stopped and clutched the footboard of his bed. "Go away! Get the fuck out of here!" Silence returned in his head. The chaotic images and thoughts were gone. He drew in a long breath, waiting to see if an attack of pain would follow. He took another deep breath, let go the bed and looked about blankly. He couldn't stay alone. He needed to be with people, others who would help hold the silence with him. He left his room quietly and went downstairs. No one was in the library, or the television room, or the breakfast room. He was on the way to the kitchen when he saw the light coming from the living room. The door was open a crack.

At last, he thought very distantly. He started toward the living room; it was like walking under water, or through a monstrous snowdrift. His body was trying to stop, his feet were weighted, his legs leaden.

Part Three

October 23

Sometimes that night Lucas was watching a recent movie on the television set, and sometimes he was watching the shows that had captivated him as a child. His father had bought one of the first TV sets in the valley at a time when the signal seemed to bounce around in the mountains and each bounce produced a new ghost. The ancient ghosts mingled with the garish color of the movie, gray shadows haunting the new stars. The volume was turned too high, adjusted deliberately by Lucas to forestall conversation, to try to drown out the voices that were clearer in his head than the voices that issued from the console. *His* grating voice, demanding, ordering, cursing; *her* voice mocking, laughing in a register a little too high; and his own childish voice whispering, "Don't fight. Please don't fight." No one had heard that plaintive voice, and hearing it now he despised the frail, frightened child he had been.

The child turned off the TV and looked for a place to hide, a place where neither of them would find him. He groaned in despair as their voices rose, *hers* not very distant.

"Did you speak?" Regina asked, begging him to speak, to say anything at all.

"I'm going to the bathroom," he said, getting up with effort. For a second or two he saw Regina, so pale she looked ill and fragile, too vulnerable. He started across the room. *She* was in the dining room now screaming furiously, drunkenly. What if he saw *her,* if *she* saw him? What if they met in the hallway? He squeezed his eyes closed knowing it was in his head, not out there, yet

afraid that the out-there and the in-here would somehow
merge, take on an enduring reality. He went into the hall
with Regina so close behind him that he could feel her
warm breath on his neck. A rush of feelings, memories,
sensations in sharp contradiction to each other threatened
to fling him into an abyss from which he would never be
able to rise again. He fought vertigo as he felt himself
running barefooted through the hallway, clutching an il-
lustrated *Connecticut Yankee*, praying *she* wouldn't leave
the dining room before he turned the corner and darted
into the living room. He wanted to stop, to take Regina into
his arms, reassure her, tell her over and over how much he
loved her, now more than ever because of her loyalty, her
courage in this insane house. And he wanted her out and
away from the house, back in New York. She had no business here, spying on him, learning things he had never
intended to tell anyone. His head ached from trying to
sort out the contradictions; it was like calling snow black,
or water dry, or hot cold. His thoughts raced out of control, opposites lined up like sames; wants became fears,
fears became needs, love became hate . . . Shame and fear
drove him up the spiral stairs, terror stopped him at the
top, suddenly aware that he might run into his father in
the plant room. At the top of the stairs his head seemed
to spin, and in the hallway leaning heavily on his crutches,
his dizziness increased. He groped for the door to the
bathroom, and was grateful for the cool glass knob that
was real, that his hand could close over, thankful that
Regina was behind him where she could not see, could
not be aware that he was losing all contact with reality,
that he was slipping away in madness. The door opened and
he nearly fell. He heard Regina gasp and he caught himself, dragged his foot and the crutches inside the bathroom,
and pushed the door hard behind him, even grateful for
the resounding slam that was also real, in present time.

Regina stared at the door, one hand outstretched as if
to test it. She drew back feeling foolish and turned to go
down to the kitchen to wait for Lucas. The kitchen was
bright, humming with appliances that gleamed, cheerful
with blue patterned tile floor, yellow daisies on the wallpaper . . . She had gone inside the room only two or three
steps when she heard the woman calling Lucas.

"Lucas, where are you?" It was a voice thick with alcohol, slurring the words.

"You can't have him, Viola!" A man's deep voice yelled back.

"Come on, honey. We're getting out of here. Where are you, Lucas?"

"Leave him alone! He stays with me. You're drunk. You'll kill yourself and him too."

"Lucas, are you in there?" She was searching. "Lucas, answer me!"

Regina knew where he was. She had seen him on the balcony, hiding under one of the plant tables near the window. He was hunched over, fetuslike, his hands crushing his ears, his eyes shut. Regina ran from the kitchen, through the hallway, into the living room, up the curved stairs, and stopped abruptly. Empty. No plants. No hiding child. She turned around and started to go down again.

Hugh entered the room and looked up to where Regina was standing on the balcony, holding a trowel in one hand, a potted plant in the other. She nodded at him, put down the plant, and started down the stairs, talking as she came.

"Froelich, are you? Read your paper. Don't believe in possession, eh? Neither do I. Neither do I . . ."

She could not stop her insane words, could not stop her descent, could not stop the flow of thoughts that were not her thoughts. He was younger than she had expected, maybe too young, too naive, too green. Maybe not as smart as she had hoped. But he would do, he had to do; he was the only fish in the waters and the season was opening right now.

She reached the bottom of the stairs, talking all the way down, and he crossed the room, staring at her in horror.

"Don't believe in coincidence . . ." her crazy voice went on. She reached out to touch him on the chest and they both saw the hand—slim and smooth, yet gnarled and brown-spotted with thick veins . . . She laughed, a dry sound of rattling bones or sticks.

She snatched her hand back and Hugh saw a look of terror transfix her and at the same time his stomach cramped so hard that he could not bear it.

Regina screamed and Hugh fell down like a dead man. The voices were everywhere, all around her, inside her. Desperately she jerked the whistle up and blew it and could not stop blowing it until someone tore it from her.

The whistle brought them all: Mallory pulling on his robe as he rushed downstairs; Conrad pushing past him,

not undressed yet; and Janet barefoot, feeling dazed, afraid
of staying on the second floor alone, more afraid of what
they would find. They grouped themselves like a wax-
worker's tableau: Mallory on one knee examining Hugh,
the others clustered around Regina. Conrad had grabbed
the whistle from her, but she had not moved yet. Lucas
was the last one to enter the room, thinking: Not Regina!
Not Regina! Please, not Regina! He was weak with relief
when he saw her unhurt, upright. Then he stopped. A
second wave of emotion hit him: fury, a rage so great he
felt himself swelling with it, felt himself expanding to fill
the room, fill the house, fill the countryside, and he wanted
to hit her, beat her senseless, and senseless, hit her again
and again. His vision blurred . . . No, he whispered to himself. Go away! Everything left him and he staggered, almost fell.

Mallory looked up and nodded briefly. Not dead, Conrad realized, with relief. He had been certain Hugh was
dead. He looked dead. Janet was shaking violently and
he put his arm around her shoulders, held her for a moment. She had thought him dead also, thought he would
now become one of the ghosts wandering the house—
laughing, mocking, taunting, whispering obscenities. Her
shaking subsided.

Mallory stood up looking at the unconscious man, and
for a moment he almost wished he had died; that would
end the madness, bring in the police who would stay the
night, keep guard. Thickly he said, "I'd better take him
to the hospital."

"Not one of us," Conrad said. "Maybe this is a trick to
get us out of the house. We all have to stay. Call Carlos."

Disappointment surged through Mallory. It would have
been a relief to get in the wagon, drive through the night,
forget the house, the will, the others. Wearily he went to
make the phone call.

Regina had not yet looked up from Hugh; she was
afraid to look away, as if he might change there on the
floor. If she did not keep the vigil, he might turn into the
old man.

Watching her, Lucas wondered how she could stay upright. She was as pale as a ghost herself. She had met
Hugh, he thought clearly, and the old man had punished
him. She was lucky he had not touched her. Next time
. . . Abruptly he turned and stumbled from the room.

Regina realized that the house was still, that the voices had been hushed by the strident whistle. She looked up and saw Lucas going through the doorway, and started after him. Conrad caught her by the arm.

"We have to know what to tell them at the hospital," he said gently. "What happened?"

She shook her head. "He just fell down, as if he had a heart attack. He didn't cry out or anything."

Conrad regarded her for a moment, then shrugged. "Okay. You and Janet go back to the television room, make yourselves a drink. We all need a drink right now. We'll be in as soon as Carlos gets here."

In Conrad's mind an image flashed: He saw Regina approaching Hugh, her hand outstretched, a look of terror transfixing her face. But it wasn't Regina. And it was he, Conrad, whom she was approaching. He closed his eyes hard, until they hurt and he saw a dull red.

When he opened his eyes he was alone with Hugh. "We're slipping in and out of each other's heads," he murmured to the unconscious man. "And frankly, old friend, I don't like it." Not only did he not like it, he thought, but it scared him beyond words. The fear was without form, abstract, so atavistic it predated language, and no words had ever been invented to describe it. Such fear must have paralyzed the earliest hominids, crouching, huddling together, staring into a black night alive with unseen presences. From such fear had arisen gods, demons, magic, and with concepts made sharable by language, those first people had shielded themselves. But the fear was still there, in the genes, waiting only for a trigger to release it, and now, as then, it was beyond words. Conrad shook his head sharply. He looked around the room, and for a moment it wavered, seemed to come undone in a curious way, as if layer by layer something was unpeeling the years, taking it back to how it had been that night . . .

Mallory returned, breathing hard, like a man at the end of a marathon run. "Carlos is on the way," he said. "And I called Sizemore. He'll arrange things at the hospital." He did not look again at Hugh, and kept his eyes averted from the balcony, thinking that if he fought it consciously, deliberately, he could keep the room from shifting, keep everything in focus. He felt as if he couldn't fill his lungs, the way he always felt when he swam underwater, almost frantic for air as soon as his head was submerged.

"Go wait with the women," Conrad said abruptly. "I don't know where Lucas took himself off to and they shouldn't be alone."

Mallory tried not to rush from the room, tried to achieve the control Conrad was displaying, but he knew his haste showed, and now, faintly, as if the speakers had been sleeping and were only half awake, he could hear their murmuring voices begin again, gathering strength, growing louder.

When Conrad joined the others in the television room Mallory put a drink in his hand. "Was he still out?"

He nodded. "Just the same." Lucas was at the table shoving stones around aimlessly, ignoring everyone. Janet was alone on a sofa, and Regina was huddled in one of the oversized chairs. Each was carefully removed from the others, separated by as much space as the room permitted, avoiding contact with anyone else. Conrad regarded Regina soberly. She was holding a glass that was nearly full, turning it around and around as if fascinated by it.

"You have to tell us what happened," Conrad said finally.

She looked up and touched the glass to her lips, but she was not drinking. She said, as if she had thought over the words carefully, chosen each one with precision, "Lucas was in the bathroom and I heard something in the living room. I was waiting in the kitchen, and I thought he might have gone out without my noticing it. I went to the living room and saw Hugh. He didn't say anything to me, just took a few steps and fell down."

"He must have heard or seen something," Mallory said heavily. "I'll go have a look around." At the door to the hallway he hesitated and took a deep breath the way a swimmer does before a dive.

Regina looked at Lucas. He was watching her, had been watching her surreptitiously ever since he had come into the television room. He didn't believe her, she knew, and was unable to think of anything she could say or do to convince him that she had not planned to meet Hugh in the living room. Lucas pretended to examine the stones, but continued to watch her, and she saw malevolence and hatred in the glances that he cast her way. It wasn't Lucas, she told herself, it was the house, the voices, his father, the past, all that, but it was not Lucas . . .

"Have you ever thought how much a car is part of the road it's traveling on?" Janet said suddenly, her face looking pinched and gray. "The road just rises and makes a lump that we call a car, and moves it along . . ."

Conrad saw it: The station wagon had reached the intersection with the highway—a lump in the road. In the back seat Hugh groaned softly, but did not stir.

Mallory yelled to them to come, and they all moved simultaneously, as if grateful for a break in the silence that had fallen over them. This time it was the sunroom plants, the fuchsias and begonias and geraniums, everything broken, scattered, uprooted. The bed had been torn apart and was bespattered with dirt and broken plants.

Janet moaned and started to weep and Regina felt as if she would vomit, the way she had felt out under the tree the day the old man had died.

"You're planning to leave me, aren't you?" Lucas demanded later in their room. Neither of them had undressed yet. Regina was laying out his robe, her gown.

"You know that's crazy," she said, going back to the closet for her slippers. "Let's not talk about anything now, not while we're in this house."

"You think I'll forget. You think after a few days go by it'll be like before, good old Luke, good old forgiving Luke with such a short memory that by Friday Monday's ancient history."

She didn't move. "Luke, don't. Not now. Not here. You know there's nothing to forgive. We have nothing to fight about, not you and me."

"Don't act dumb! For Christ's sake, just don't act dumb! I'm going down and keep watch with Connie. I'll sleep on the sofa."

"Lucas, stop it! When we get away from here, you'll know you're being unfair. It isn't you talking."

She could see the changes happening on his face, the look of disgust and hatred, chased by bewilderment and fear, that in turn became fury . . . He hobbled out, dragging his foot.

Reluctantly she followed him, too afraid to stay alone in the bedroom, even more afraid to leave Lucas by himself if Conrad should fall asleep. Now the house rustled and murmured and breathed as doors opened and closed; footsteps pounded on the stairs; something crashed and broke in the kitchen. Resolutely she kept her attention focused on Lucas and ignored the sounds.

Conrad seemed not at all surprised to see them and they tried to arrange themselves in the chairs, on the sofa, to rest and pretend to sleep. No one talked, but the air was filled with voices. Regina lay back in a reclining chair with an afghan spread over her and watched the fire, now and then turning her gaze to Lucas who stretched out on the sofa. He stared at the ceiling.

She thought again of what Janet had said: The road rises in a lump that moves along and we call it a car. She had read that one of the common nightmares shared universally was of the earth rising, forming itself into lumpish figures, peoplelike creatures without details who moved along sluggishly, noiselessly, and were terrifying to behold. In her mind's eye other forms arose from the ground: mountains, trees, animals. They emerged in rough shapes and painfully finished themselves, took on life of their own. She dreamed: A beautiful woman was running toward her laughing, saying in a singsong voice: "We'll go to New York, just you and me. You'll become a famous painter and your work will hang in the Metropolitan. You'll paint dozens of portraits of me and they'll all hang in the Metropolitan!" Regina smelled the alcohol on her breath and she could see the slack mouth, the red-rimmed eyes, the mascara that had been smeared. She ducked the kiss the woman tried to give her.

"Regina, wake up," Conrad said, shaking her gently. "You were dreaming."

She sat up with a start. Lucas was not in the room.

"He's gone to get a sandwich or something. He'll be right back. Are you all right now?"

She nodded. For a moment his voice reminded her of her father, and she wished she could call him, talk to him, describe the house, the people . . .

"You love your father very much," Conrad said. "Lucky you."

She stared at him.

"He's medium height, a scar on his chin from . . . a golf club that someone let fly. Greenish eyes . . ."

"Stop," she whispered. "How do you know?"

"I don't know. Maybe no one is going to have any hidden self before this is all over. I'm going to answer with the exact truth anything anyone asks me from now on. Will you do the same?"

She shook her head. "I don't know. What does all this mean?"

"I'm not sure. I think Hugh knows, but he'd rather die with stomach cramps than talk about it. He'll never take the truth pledge."

"You figured that out? That he's doing it to himself?"

"I didn't figure it out," he said slowly. "But I know."

Her skin turned icy with his words, and she pulled the afghan closer around her.

"The same way I know about your father, and the same way I know about Luke's mother that last night."

"And what about your wife, Karen? What do you suppose we'll all know about you and her before this is done?" Lucas demanded from the doorway. He sounded ugly, his voice harsh and biting.

"You already know or you wouldn't bring it up," Conrad said. "I hit her and she left me. I hit Betty Jo too and she left me."

"Just like him! Only you didn't have the guts to do a thorough job."

"Just like him," Conrad murmured. "I kept thinking so. I thought it was the only way to treat women. He taught us all how to handle women, didn't he, Luke?"

"I never hit a woman in my life!"

"Not yet. Not yet." Conrad went to the fireplace and poked at the log, made it blaze high. "I saw you tonight, Luke. I know what you were thinking. I know how the crutch felt in your hand."

"He wouldn't!" Regina cried.

Lucas looked at her for a long time without speaking. He limped to a chair and sat down. "I might," he said almost in a whisper. "I wanted to. It was all I could think of, how much I wanted to beat you, knock you down, hurt you real bad. When I thought you had gone off to be with Hugh, that's all I could think of, hitting you. I don't want to be alone with you again. I'm afraid to be alone with you. Not until this is over."

Regina jumped up from her chair and flung the cover aside. She ran to Lucas and took his hand; it was cold and unresisting. "But you didn't hit me. You couldn't. That wasn't you thinking those things. It's the house. I'm not afraid of you, Lucas. You're sweet and gentle and kind, not like him. You are not like him!"

"Not like," he said with a strange smile. "At times this week, too many times, I've been him. He's after me, Regina. He's decided. Maybe I'm the weakest one, the least able to resist, or something. I don't know why. But he's after me." He withdrew his hand. "I've seen Connie as a little kid, and Mallory, for God's sake! I know how Mallory ran around the house when he was three, four years old!"

"He's after all of us!" Regina said dully. "Even me."

"All of us," Conrad echoed. "Maybe Hugh was right and we're all under some kind of compulsion to act out this scenario his way. Maybe it's all a mass hallucination or a mass hypnotic spell. It's not just you, kid. Believe me, it isn't just you."

"After it's over, we'll have a vacation," Regina said. "We'll rest and sleep a lot and play. This will fade away like a nightmare. Lucas? Please, just look at me!"

He was staring into the distance, his face twisted in a grimace like a caricature of a smile. "I won't leave," he said. "I told you. He's decided and I'm it. I won't be able to leave. I'll . . . I'll . . ."

"What, Luke?" Conrad asked. "You'll do what?"

"Never mind. Nothing. Let's get some rest."

Regina saw him again on the bluff overlooking the river, saw his resolution, and the steady movement toward the edge; she felt her own impact against him as she lunged, and then they were both tumbling, slipping . . . She knew what he would do. On the bluff, again at the beach on a cliff she had seen that look, had felt that same resolve.

"Let's leave now," she cried, "tonight, this minute. We can borrow a car and drive into town. Lucas, we were happy without money. We were! You know it."

Lucas leaned his head back against the chair and closed his eyes, the curious smile on his lips. They always wanted to go to town. It was always like that.

His mother had come in to tell him good night. She was going to town, dressed in a long pale dress that gleamed like moonlight on the grass, and she smelled like spicy, forbidden flowers. When she leaned over to kiss him, he could see her breasts, almost to the nipples, and the sight, the fragrance had made him dizzy. She was a fairy princess, the most beautiful in the world, going out to the ball where she would meet a handsome prince and they would go away together, and take him with them, and they would all live happily, dancing and singing and eating splendid fruits . . .

"Just where the hell do you think you're going?" *His* voice came from the open door.

"Sleep well, honey," she said to Lucas and left the bedroom; her gown seemed to whisper secrets when she moved. He tried to see if she wore glass slippers, but he could not tell. He crept from bed and opened the door a crack to watch his mother and father in the hallway.

"I told you, I'm going to Eddie's party. Just because you don't like parties doesn't mean I can't go."

"It's too foggy. It's going to be freezing within the hour. And it isn't a party. It's a drunken gambling carouse. You're better off burning up your money in the fireplace."

"If it's too bad, I'll stay in town overnight."

"It's too bad to start."

"Don't be a fool, John. You always want to build a fence around your possessions, and with most of them that's fine, but not with me. I won't stay cooped up in this house month after month after month. If you have a pretty bird, you have to let it fly."

"You're not going," he said evenly. "I have the keys, and the only way you'll leave this house tonight is by flying, or on foot. No more gambling. No more boozing." He went into his room and closed the door, leaving her in the hallway. She groped in her purse, a tiny golden bag, and threw it at his door. She ran to the stairs and down, out of sight of Lucas. Now he left his room and raced through the hallway to the balcony where he sat behind the railing and watched the living room. After several minutes she appeared with a glass in her hand. She picked up the phone and dialed, jiggled the receiver up and down several times, and then threw it across the room, as far as the cord would reach. She drained her glass and hurled it against the wall. Lucas scurried back to his room and burrowed down into his bedding. He pulled the covers over his head, tucking them in all around him, as if he thought that by being in a cocoon he would be safe from the fight that was now inevitable.

So beautiful, he thought. So goddam beautiful. His fingers twitched as he thought of her lovely breasts, the skin like clouds that you could sink into.

He jerked his eyes open. He had slept after all. Regina

was asleep on the reclining chair and Conrad was dozing in the deep chair by the fire. The light was pale gray; morning had come finally. Lucas was stiff with cold and his whole leg throbbed when he shifted his position. The house was very quiet. The deep hush of dawn lay over the house, over the yard.

He tried to remember a dream, gave it up and regarded Regina. How childlike she appeared, a little girl who had fallen asleep watching television perhaps. Tender hands had arranged the cover over her, taking care not to awaken her, and now she slept softly, her breath so gentle it was hard to see any movement. Leave her alone, he thought fiercely then. Just leave her alone. Take me if you want. I deserve it, but leave her alone! There was no answer in the still house.

Everyone was tired that morning. Mallory was on the phone for an hour talking first to Strohm, then to Sizemore, and finally to a resident doctor at Salem General Hospital. "They'll make the EEGs," he announced. "They want us in at eleven. They have a neurologist who can compare them all this afternoon." He looked ill and very old. "Hugh's being released this morning after some tests. He seems okay."

"Someone has to get the first ones from Hugh," Janet said. "Maybe you can, Regina, while we're having the next bunch made."

Regina nodded. It did not matter. Go see Hugh, run errands, sit in a hospital waiting room, it made little difference to her. There was no question of her remaining alone in the house while the rest of them went to town. One more day, she kept thinking. One more day. One more night. At first she had been convinced that they could stand anything for so few days and nights, but now . . . One more night. The phrase ran through her head over and over. There was no conversation on the way to Salem. They went in two cars, Mallory and Lucas in the station wagon, Conrad and the two women in his car. Regina would drive Conrad's car to Corvallis to collect the first set of electroencephalograms.

This morning it seemed crazy to talk about the road forming a lump and moving it along, Regina thought, watching the fields, the tall dark firs, men in the apple orchard with ladders. All separate, all distinct, each thing, each person individual. Last night it had not seemed so insane.

She went to Hugh's room in the hospital, where he was waiting for his release forms, the nurse told her. He was standing at the window, tapping on the sill, as rigid as a tree himself. He whirled around when she entered through the open door.

"I thought it was that damn intern," he said sourly. "What are you doing here?"

"They need the first EEGs, for the next step. They're having another set made this morning."

"They can't have them."

"You can't refuse. You agreed. They'll just get a court order or something. They have to fulfill the terms of the will."

"Court order? You're right. Strohm's such a jackass, that's his style. Come on. They're in Corvallis."

"You can't leave, can you? I thought you had to wait for a release or something."

"Watch me. Let's go."

He looked feverish, hyper, and so tight that she feared he might topple if he got off balance even a little.

"Hugh, are you well enough? I could pick them up."

He glanced at her and shrugged. "Come on. You have to drive. My car's still out at the farm." He led the way and she followed without further protests.

He directed her to the highway, south to Corvallis, and through the streets lined with horse chestnut trees that were so large and wide they turned each street into a tunnel. She asked no questions and he remained silent except for his brusque orders to turn at the next corner, take a left, third house on the right . . .

She followed him inside his house, to his office. She had not entered this room when she and Lucas had stayed here. Now she looked about with curiosity. Tiny, hardly big enough for an extra chair, it seemed to reflect him in all ways, from the jumble of papers and notebooks on the desk in what looked like random heaps to the calendar on the wall, so marked up it was hard to see the number of days. He unlocked a file cabinet and took out a thick folder. He didn't open it or glance at it, but tucked it under his arm and slammed the drawer shut, locked it again. All his motions were swift and jerky, like a puppet being manipulated by an inept master.

"I'll take them back," she said, reaching for the folder.

"I'm going to burn them," he said sharply. "No one takes them back."

"You can't! Hugh, let me have them! It wouldn't be fair to make them go through this week and not be able to finish it. You are sick. You should go to bed, get some rest. Please, let me have them." Burn them, she thought. That was the answer. Just burn them up and be done with them. But then they might have to stay another week, do it all over again. She felt cold. The thought of delaying the end of this madness, or having the will invalidated, new requirements being ordered, lent force to her voice as she continued in a rush. "Aren't you even curious to learn if there's been a change? What would it mean if they've changed?"

"They've changed," he said. "All of them."

"Please, let's sit down and talk a minute. Conrad says you know what's happening in that house. Do you?"

He shook his head.

"You do though. What happened to me last night? What happened to you? Lucas is convinced that his father is trying to possess him, that he's succeeding. He's going to kill himself. I know he is. And you can help him, help all of us. You can't just turn your back on us now." There was desperation in her voice and she was near tears. Angrily she turned away from him and took a deep breath. He made no response and when she faced him again, he was staring fixedly at the wall; she reached out and touched his arm. "Hugh?"

He blinked rapidly. "You're right," he said. "It's my responsibility. I keep trying to pretend it isn't. If that old bastard hadn't read my paper, if he hadn't talked to me those nights, he wouldn't have done this. It's my fault. He wouldn't have thought of this in a million years by himself. Synchronicity. He was looking for something and I came along with that fucking paper."

"What is he doing? For God's sake, what is he *doing?"*

"Nothing. He's dead. He can't do anything ever again."

It was mechanical, the recitation of a lesson memorized without comprehension. His voice was dull; there was no hope there.

"What happened last night? I was that old man coming downstairs! I should have been riding down in a seat of some sort. I could feel it. And those things I said. That's what he said to you, isn't it? When you first met. I remembered it. All of it. What happened?" Her voice rose in spite of her effort to remain calm, to be reasonable. The events of last night were like the lump in the road; they had seemed possible, but today it should all be explainable, even laughable.

"You were hysterical. So was I. Hypersuggestibility, that explains everything going on in that house, everything."

"No," she said. "That explains nothing. I was that old man! That was how you first met, I know it." She took a deep breath and went on in a rush. "In the beginning we were all separate, individual, and then we began to see things, to hear things that weren't our own memories, as if barriers were being broken down. It's as if we should have invisible shells around ourselves, impenetrable shells, and the shells are being dissolved, stripped away, and we have no more protection. I've known what you were seeing; I've felt what Lucas felt as a child . . . And always *he's* there, showing us his past . . . We can't stand it any longer, Hugh! None of us can stand this! We'll all go insane!"

He seemed to freeze as she spoke; his expression was so cold, so distant that she felt chilled by him, the way she would feel chilled standing too close to a glacier.

"You're hysterical," he said distinctly. "You're not even trying to be rational. You're acting like a silly adolescent girl caught up in mass hysteria. Come on, we'd better get back before Lucas begins to worry."

Her chill deepened. Now it was an icy fury that she felt. Her shell was intact, as was his. From her earliest childhood she had been trained not to ask for help, to be self-sufficient, to be self-reliant, and now when she had forced herself to reach out for help, she had been rebuffed so thoroughly that she could feel only hatred for him.

"Just give me the folder," she said. "If you won't help us, tell us what you know, just stay out of it. We don't want you there."

"That's our dilemma, Regina, yours and mine. We're not part of it, but we have to be there. We can't go back and we have to." He was an ice man, remote, unreachable, unknowable.

He went to the door. She hung back; her feet refused to move. He had said it. She couldn't deliberately go back to that house, to the voices, the rustlings. She couldn't go back to watch Lucas shift and become a stranger in an instant, see fury and madness redden his eyes, etch deep lines on the sides of his mouth.

"You do love him, don't you," Hugh said without inflection. He paused at the door looking at her dispassionately.

"You know I do."

"Let's go then. I'll tell you a story while you drive."

She felt her heart skip, then race, and her mouth went dry. Now he would tell her, and she was not certain she wanted him to after all. She was more afraid of his explanation than of the mystery.

"It's a myth," he said, as she backed out the driveway. "Once, before there was time, free-roaming spirits began to cruise the universe, and to create things—a star here, a planetoid there, a galaxy. It was fun for a while, but everything was still lifeless. One by one they began to inhabit their creations, animate them. For some of them this was a holy mission, for others it was a diversion, for still others, an art form, and so on. Or perhaps they were all simple experiments, the kind a schoolboy does when he grows a culture of bacteria in a Petri dish."

She glanced at him, sick with frustration and disappointment. He was staring straight ahead, rigid, immobile. She drove faster, wanting to hurry the day, to race through it, find herself in tomorrow. One more day. One more night.

"One of them made a solar system and selected a planet for itself. It began to create, of course. Mountains, rivers, oceans, life of all sorts. Finally it decided to give its life forms intelligence, maybe to amuse itself. Who knows? You're driving too fast."

"And you're dressing up Bible stories."

"With a difference." He held up his hands and wriggled his fingers. "You ever play with those little finger puppets?" He crooked a finger and said in a falsetto, "My name is Max. As for you, Wilberforce, take that!" The finger rapped the forefinger of his other hand sharply. "Watch the road," he said, and he clenched his fists, let them rest on his knees.

"I don't know what you're trying to tell me," Regina said, slowing down. "Just say it, whatever it is."

"You have to imagine the little heads, their tiny eyes, minuscule brains, invisible egos," he said softly. "And the wee little dresses and suits. The question is, should Wilberforce hold the attack against Max? Should Max have a bad conscience for attacking without provocation?" He laughed, but his fists remained tight.

Crazy, crazy! She gripped the wheel harder. She had seen a magician perform a finger puppet show once in grade school. Joe and Harry, two clowns alone on a table-top world. Joe had rolled a log in Harry's path, and Harry had stumbled over it, falling flat on his nose, time after time. The magician had been sitting on the floor, his chin resting on the table as he watched his puppets on his fore-fingers, both of them bowing, nodding. He had put them down on the table and turned his back, as if to go on to another part of the show, and they had followed him across the tabletop, and both of them had fallen over the log. She remembered the squeals of delight and surprise and the magician's feigned ignorance of the cause. Finally the au-dience had gotten through to him, that he should look at his puppets. He had been surprised. He had replaced the puppets on the center of the table and left again, and the incident had been repeated. Then he had put the two little clowns in his pocket, and during the rest of the show, from time to time one or the other had poked his head out, as if looking for something. Each time, the magician had shoved it back down.

In her head Regina heard the question: What would have happened if Harry and Joe had found out that neither of them had been responsible for the falls, the humiliation, the pain?

"Regina, we'll arrive by ambulance if you keep this up," Hugh said quietly, and she felt his hand on her arm. She was driving on the shoulder, doing eighty-five. His hand was firm and warm; she could feel the warmth through her sweater.

He talked as she got the car back on the road, slowing down to forty-five, which she held the rest of the way. He talked about the apple crop, about the fertile valley that could grow two, sometimes three, crops a year. He kept his hand on her arm for only a moment or two, and it was as if that gesture had relaxed him even more than her, for after that he looked and acted almost normal with no more sign of the rigidity that had made him a stranger only minutes before. The vast distance she had sensed was now more like a normal detachment or preoccupation.

Very soon they arrived at the hospital where they found Janet in the coffee shop.

"Ladies first and all that," she said, indicating the upper part of the building with her thumb. "How are you?" she asked Hugh.

"Okay. They did tests, we'll know later."

"You've got those things?" She was looking at the folder.

"I'll compare them myself," he said. "Part of the deal." She nodded. "How? Will you do it here?"

"Just a visual scan here. Then we'll put them all in the computer for analysis. That will take a while, depending on computer time."

"We won't know right away then. Not before tomorrow?"

"I doubt it. We'll see."

She slumped. "God, it goes on and on. Did he know how long this part would take?"

"Oh yes. He knew exactly how long."

She closed her eyes and took a deep breath. "I can feel him pulling strings, tugging this way and that, anticipating our every move. His sense of timing was perfect, you know. He was an artist really, more than I ever was, or Luke either. Take a look out any window of that house and you see a perfect composition, perfect in every detail. An artist working with living material, trees, grass, flowers. He planned his masterwork at the farm, every detail in place, accounted for. He was a genius, I suppose."

"He was insane at the end," Hugh said remotely.

Regina stared at him. "You said before that he wasn't."

"I was wrong. He was crazy, this whole scheme is crazy."

"Do you still think we're doing everything to ourselves?" Janet asked with a touch of malice.

"Yes. He understood each of you thoroughly and none of you understood him at all. You were all kids when you left home, but he kept track of you. He knew Mallory had to come without his wife. Why?"

"She's an earnest, pragmatic, religious fundamentalist without a trace of humor or mysticism," Janet said promptly. "She would have had the police in to stand guard after the first plants were smashed."

Hugh nodded. "He knew that Lucas needed Regina. He knew it would be better if I stayed. He was a genius, but even geniuses get hooked on ideas that are lunatic. He did, and everything that follows from that insane premise is equally insane."

"Will the EEGs prove anything?"

"They'll prove he was wrong. There is no mechanism that allows for possession, and I'll prove it with the results of today's tests."

Janet was watching him closely, as if puzzled by him, his new air of detachment. "I pray to God that you can."

And Regina, watching him also, thought he was lying. He was as frightened as he had been before, but now he was hiding it, pretending confidence she didn't believe in. His fingers were tapping, tapping.

He had to invent theories, she realized. He had to detach himself and explain in words things that could never be explained. His lifetime of training, his years working as a psychologist, his entire belief system forced him to deny anything that did not fit neatly into an accepted scheme. She remembered an argument she had had in one of her psychology classes in which she had taken the position that in every work of art there exists a part of the artist. Shakespeare lives in his works, Beethoven in his music, Rubens, Gauguin . . . "I suppose we should look for noses, elbows, fingernails perhaps . . ." the teacher had said sarcastically. But it was true then, she told herself, and it was true now. Culbertson had created a work of art, not simply the house, but the entire farm, and he was there, would always be there. The ashes could be washed away, even if there were no ashes, he would be there forever, as long as the trees endured, as long as the stream tumbled from the mountain . . . Whoever had smashed the flowerpots, mutilated the roses and dahlias had lashed out at the old man, knowing intuitively that he was there. And, she thought, he has found the power somehow to melt away our protective walls, to expose us to each other, to destroy the safety of our separateness.

Later, going back to the farm, Janet and Conrad began to tell stories about an impossible dog they had had. She had eaten a garden hose, and a two-by-four, and a hot pepper plant, peppers and all . . . As they all laughed, Regina thought, what a relief, and how unexpected. Hugh was wrong, she found herself thinking: Their father had never predicted a human reaction in his life beyond the most obvious. His wives and children had all eluded his understanding completely. Following that came another, more sobering realization: In life he had tried to dominate them all, tried to manipulate them, force them to his will, and

he had failed time and again. Then escape had been possible. Lucas had run away; Conrad had left home, as had
Janet. Mallory had moved out very young. Now they were
all trapped, past events were being telescoped in an accel-
erating time frame and no one, least of all the father, could
have predicted the reactions of his children. Just as he had
misjudged people all his life, he had continued to mis-
judge them with the writing of his insane will, and even
after death. And Hugh knew all that, she thought.

Hugh had not made a simple mistake, he had lied deliberately and convincingly. He had to lie, she realized, because he was perhaps even more afraid than she was.

When they reached the farm, Mallory's wagon was already
parked in the driveway. Regina took a deep breath and
opened the back door to get out; she glanced at Conrad
and Janet who were not yet moving.

"Go on. We'll be along in a minute," Conrad said.

She did not want to. She wanted to sit in the car all
day, curl up on the back seat and sleep there that night.
She started to walk to the porch. Such a beautiful house,
such beautiful grounds; it truly was a work of art, perfect
in every detail. She turned to look across the deep yard, to
the fence posts, all white, with invisible fencing that she
assumed was wire. A perfect composition, lovely colors—
greens, white, the red road, the white picked up by the
sheep, deeper greens, almost blacks of the towering fir trees,
and over there the graceful curves of a spruce . . . Perfect
composition. The winter wheat was vivid green against the
black earth . . . When it ripened it would be golden, alive
in the wind, and over there the gold would be picked up by
low-growing daisies, picked up, enriched, and the red of
the lava repeated in the red barn rising massively from a
bed of clover that would be like tiny sheep . . .

"Regina!"

She started violently and turned to see Lucas framed by
the doorway, leaning on one crutch.

"You looked like a sleepwalker," he said. "What's
wrong?"

"Nothing." She hurried into the house and was met by
a surging, bodiless flood of people, happenings, voices.

As she rushed inside, Lucas remembered. He had been
trying and trying to recall when he had changed, when he
had stopped loving his mother blindly, when he had be-

come critical and had decided not to go away with her and her prince charming. Just like this, he thought clearly. She had come home and stopped on the porch, and she had thrown up. The man with her had cursed and shoved her inside the house and, cursing, had left, roared down the driveway in a long, pale blue car.

"Lucas, what are you doing down here? It's past your bedtime. Go on, get upstairs." She had reached for him and missed as he sidestepped, and she had fallen down, right here, where Regina was standing, swaying back and forth, her eyes tightly closed.

He had known all at once that there was no prince charming. She was not a princess. It was a lie, all of it. He had run upstairs and flung himself down on his bed to sob wildly, muffling the noise in his pillow.

He had forgotten that, Lucas thought in wonder. He had forgotten until this moment. He looked at the floor almost expecting to see her lying there. He could smell the sour vomit odor, and the alcohol. Her dress had been torn, or maybe it had simply been dirty.

Regina moaned softly, and he reached out for her, held her so hard that she could not breathe. "My God," she whispered. "Oh, my God! I saw Viola, Lucas. I saw her."

"Hush," he said softly. "Sh. It's all right. It's over. It's quiet now." He continued to hold her, and that was how Conrad and Janet found them a minute later.

Conrad nodded. "Where's Mallory? TV room?" He and Janet went around Lucas and Regina.

"Okay?" Lucas asked.

She nodded.

"Let's go have a bite of something," he said. "There's a buffet in the television room. We told Anita no one wanted a real lunch today. Okay with you?"

Again she nodded. They walked slowly to the room where the others were already having sandwiches. Lucas kept his arm around her shoulders, and she thought, it would be all right. If they were together, if he did not exclude her, it would be all right.

"I say we should all get the hell out of here and stay out until midnight," Conrad said as they entered the room. "I'm taking Janet to town and later we'll have dinner and maybe see a movie or something. We'll be back before twelve."

Mallory nodded. He looked at Lucas, glanced at his leg. "You up to a day out?"

"Where?"

"A ride up in the mountains, maybe up to Timberline Lodge. We can get a reservation for dinner. There's been a foot of snow already, should be a pretty drive."

Lucas shrugged. "Sure. If you're not too tired."

"It's set then," Mallory said with new energy in his voice, as if the thought of leaving the house was enough in itself to revitalize him. They all ate quickly and then scattered to get ready. There was an almost feverish excitement in the air as if they were schoolchildren playing hooky.

"You never go into the mountains without survival gear," Mallory said cheerfully, a few minutes later, dumping an armload of jackets and hats and gloves on the sofa.

When they were nearly ready to leave, Regina found that she was holding her breath, afraid the house would still forbid this outing, that something would happen that would make them stay. The house maintained its preternatural silence, and only when the station wagon made the turn on the lava road did Regina believe they were actually free for the rest of the day. She turned halfway around in the front seat to smile at Lucas who was sitting crosswise on the middle seat. He grinned back at her, sharing her relief. Like jailbirds who have crossed the barbed wire fence, he thought; she nodded and abruptly turned around again to stare out the windshield. Only to find another fence, higher, and beyond it another, she thought, and strangely, the thought sounded like Lucas's voice in her ear.

Mallory talked about the valley, protected from the Pacific storms by the coast range, protected from the bitter arctic cold fronts by the Cascades, bathed in mist and gentle rains all winter, yielding a bounty that was so plentiful that the Indians who had lived here had felt no need to roam, no need to learn ways to store food, no need to eye with envy any living creature. He talked about the fruits: apples, cherries, peaches, apricots, plums . . . the bush fruits, the nuts, the fields of grasses, winter wheat, the corn that was harvestable until late October year after year . . . He should get it, Regina thought suddenly; he loves this land as much as his father, as much as a man could love it. It should be his. He glanced at her as if she had spoken, an enquiring look on his face. She shook her head; her hands clenched in her lap began to hurt as her fingernails bit in. She opened them and looked out the side window. They were climbing through deep forests, so thick there was perpetual twilight back from the road. Along the sides of the road every surface was green with ferns and mosses.

She saw a pocket of snow in a sheltered spot, then another, then a meadow with a scattering of snow, and finally they were in skiing country and Lucas and Mallory reminisced about cross-country skiing jaunts they had had years ago. Mallory rounded a sharp curve slowly and pulled into a lookout parking space and they sat without talk, watching the sunset. From here it seemed they could see the entire valley, a mosaic of green and black, with a golden wash over everything. The golden light became pink, then violet, and the sky was streaked with crimson and cobalt blue. When the colors faded, Mallory pulled on to the road again and drove on.

For the first time since leaving their apartment in New York Regina felt at peace. Such beauty, she thought, and although she knew there was a very complicated ending to the thought, she could not form it, could not keep her mind at it long enough to put into words the way the startlingly beautiful sunset had made her feel. Protective of the valley, the mountains, proud, happy, at peace, all that and more. Awe, she decided. She had felt awed and almost holy for a moment. And more, she had felt at home, as if she had always known that moment was the only important moment, and everything she did that was not of that moment was an interruption, even if it meant her entire life made up that interruption. She still felt dissatisfied with the language she was using to try to capture the feeling; if she did not use language to classify it, to file it away, and later to retrieve it, it would be lost, she knew, and yet the language was wrong, inadequate. Perhaps no language had been invented or developed for something like this, and it had to remain formless and elusive because there were no words to wrap around it ...

"There's the lodge," Mallory said, breaking the silence that had lasted ever since they had left the lookout.

Beside him, Regina tried one more time to catch her own feelings, to remember, but already they were dimming and what she remembered was that there had been something, now gone, that had been important to keep.

It was eleven-thirty-five when Mallory pulled up before the Culbertson house again. Every window glowed with light; Mallory had gone through switching on lamps before leaving so that no one would have to enter a dark house.

They all remained unmoving, looking at the house. Regina had dozed the last hour of the trip. She felt very wide awake now. What conversation they had attempted on the way back had dwindled and faded away entirely during the descent from the lodge, and now they looked silently at the house. Conrad's car was not in sight.

"Well," Mallory said. He had turned off the lights and had removed the key already; it was as if each of them waited for someone else to fumble with the car door first. Mallory did, opened his door, turning on the dome light, and Lucas and Regina finally moved also.

As they approached the front door, it swung open to reveal a man standing there. Regina stifled a scream and Mallory cursed under his breath.

"Sorry," Hugh Froelich said from the open door. "Didn't mean to startle you." He moved aside to allow them to enter. "I came out by taxi and the driver was already gone before I realized the house was empty. I still had Janet's key and I just came on in."

"You've been here alone?" Mallory asked.

Hugh nodded. "I've been reading. I hope you don't mind."

The house was quiet, no rustlings, no whispers, no shrieks or laughter. Regina looked at Hugh fearfully. He was cold and distant, so proper and polite that it was as if he were acting a part in a play, not at all involved with them, with the house.

"There's Conrad's car," Hugh said, as they entered. He had not closed the door yet; they could see the headlights as the car went up over the bridge, vanished behind the shrubbery, then appeared again, closer.

They continued to stand huddled near the door, as if afraid that by moving on into the house they would awaken the voices. When Conrad and Janet drew near, Mallory took a deep breath and started to walk down the hallway. Come on, he thought, you sons of bitches! I know you're just waiting. Come on! The silence was undisturbed.

"I'll get some ice," he muttered. "Be in the television room." He marched now, wanting the confrontation, unwilling to endure the silence, which was becoming even more oppressive than the voices.

"I looked for you in the hospital," Conrad said, joining the group by the door, addressing Hugh.

"Oh? I was in one of the conference rooms upstairs."

"I know where you were. They told me. The door was locked. I pounded loud enough to get thrown out."

"I didn't hear you," Hugh said coolly. "Maybe I had already left."

"You were there," Conrad said and moved on past him. He paused, listening, then shrugged.

Janet also stopped to listen. She was very tired, at the point of exhaustion that could send her into hysterics, or a weeping fit, or, in the old days, a bout of eating. She clutched her handbag tighter and followed Conrad. She hated the silence more than anything else, she thought. She remembered wandering the house as a girl, when everything was dark, everyone else sleeping, and even then she had hated the silence, had found herself holding her breath trying to hear anything at all, a clock ticking, the wind beyond the windows, a board creaking, anything. She let out a deep breath when she realized that now she had been holding it just as she had done then.

Regina tightened her grasp of Lucas's hand and he returned the pressure. Children afraid of the dark, she thought, that's what we all are. Just children afraid of the dark. Afraid if we hear anything, afraid if we don't. She glanced at Hugh standing at the door looking outside. He closed the door and turned, and for a moment her gaze and his locked and she felt overcome by terror, as if she had glimpsed a monster. He strode past her and Lucas and she watched his back.

"Come on," Lucas said. "Let's get it over with. Hear him out."

In the television room Mallory was seated at the desk with one of the ledgers open although he was not even pretending to read it. Conrad was mixing drinks; Janet was sitting near the fire that Hugh had made earlier. She looked frozen.

"I'll stick to coffee," Hugh said when Conrad looked at him questioningly.

"You're staying the night, old buddy?"

"Yes. Down here."

Conrad turned to Lucas. "Bourbon, gin, vodka . . ."

"Nothing. Later maybe."

Conrad took his glass and sat on a straight chair that he pulled close to Hugh's chair. "Okay, Professor, tell us. What did you find?"

"Nothing that wasn't entirely predictable. Everyone has changed somewhat, not enough sleep, too much anxiety, and so on. It all shows. For instance, no one was able to achieve the alpha state, the relaxation wave. The changes seem to be in the range of four or five percent, hardly significant."

"Are any of them like his?" Janet asked.

"Absolutely not. His brain waves were those of an old man. It's a distinct pattern, just as an infant's pattern is distinct, and an adolescent's. The brain never stops changing. None of yours are anything like his."

Lucas exhaled noisily through his mouth.

"Can we double-check that?" Janet demanded. She was leaning forward in her chair watching him.

"Sure. I turned them all over to the psych lab at the university. The computer will do a very detailed comparison and analysis. What I did today was a simple visual scan, but I'm certain of the results. It'll take them a day or two. I told them to rush it."

Lying, Regina thought. He expected them to forget the whole thing after the following day. He was counting on it. She closed her eyes and for a moment she saw him leaning over a long table that was covered with papers, the EEGs, frowning at them in disbelief, or surprise, or anger, making notes . . . She jerked as the scene went black, as if she had fallen asleep and lost her entire visual field all at once. When she opened her eyes Hugh was looking at her with his stranger's eyes. She flinched and turned away.

"There's your paper," Janet said, relaxing back into her chair now. "Proof your theory's right, all that. A feather in your cap, Professor."

"I told you I won't write a paper about this."

"Right," Conrad said. "Let's have our drinks and then off to bed. I told Sizemore no one's sleeping very well, and kindly gentle heart that he is, he prescribed pills, safe for everyone, guaranteed for one good night's sleep. I think he's afraid we'll call him out again, and he's fed up with us all."

He put a small bottle of pills on the table. He was whistling under his breath the melody from an old nonsense song that he had not thought about for years. One time his junior high school choir had sung it at a program for parents. "This old man, he played one, he played knick-knack on my thumb . . ." He was holding his drink and his fingers tightened so much they hurt when he thought suddenly, *not like his, but like each other's* . . . In one after another of the EEGs the peaks and valleys coincided. In his head he heard Hugh Froelich's voice: "Give the dog a bone, this old man is coming home." The tune started again, faster now, like a tape loop in his mind, over and over and over. He drank deeply and then looked at Hugh who was regarding him without expression. "With a knick-knack paddywhack," Conrad said out loud. Hugh looked blank, like a man sleeping with his eyes open.

"Guess I won't have a pill," Conrad said and went to sit down again, hearing the song going on. "Think I'll stay down here and keep you company, Professor."

"Lucas, let's stay up too," Regina said quickly. "I'm too keyed up to even want to go to bed. After the will is read in the morning we can go to a motel and sleep around the clock."

Lucas nodded. "Stay together, that's the way." He glanced at his watch. "Not too much left of the night."

Suddenly Mallory slammed the ledger shut, the sound was as explosive as a rifle shot. He swiveled his chair around and looked out the window, seeing the rise of the hills that grew into mountains, a natural boundary of his farm, heavily forested, carpeted with green moss.

"That timber's not to be clear-cut," he said hoarsely. "Leave a scar up there, pollute the river. I won't have it! It's self-perpetuating if you do it right, no more than two percent a year, and no slash to be left behind. Carry the trash out, goddam it! Been like that for fifteen years, be like that forever . . ."

Janet screamed.

Regina covered her face with both hands. If she started to scream, she knew she would not be able to stop. It did not matter if they were together, if they were wide awake, whatever they did. Here in this room with all of them together, he was among them, and talking to them, telling them what they had to do, now and forever.

As if they had needed a scream to rouse them, the voices started again, all of them from all over the house joined in a cacophony that was an insult to the ears. Janet burst into loud sobs.

Conrad jumped up and smashed his glass against the stone fireplace. "Stop it!" he screamed ferociously. At the same time Hugh crossed the room to the hall door and closed it firmly. He pressed his forehead against it. The room became quiet again although they all knew the halls were full of sounds, the halls, the other rooms, the balcony. It was like a television set with the sound turned so low it was almost subliminal.

October 24

HUGH MADE THEM play cards. He and Conrad arranged
the table and chairs; Lucas swept the rocks away into a
bag and wiped the tabletop, and Mallory searched out
cards and chips.

"I have no money," Regina said, straining to hear beyond the door, to learn if they were still out there.

"Your credit's good as gold," Hugh said, counting out
chips. He had appointed himself banker. When they all
had chips he picked up the cards and began to deal. "Five
cards, one-eyed jacks wild. Draw."

Hugh and Conrad began making up games when the
deal got to them, and the games became wilder, silly games
that made the others laugh in disbelief when the rules
were outlined seriously.

"One-eyed king, queen of hearts, and deuces wild,"
Conrad said. "Seven cards and if you can't bet you have
to pass a card to the person on your left."

Lucas groaned. "I need to keep notes."

Janet repeated the rules verbatim and studied her cards.
She was a winner so far. The coffeepot was empty but no
one suggested that they should go make more. No one had
touched the liquor again. The cards began to blur before
Regina's eyes and it seemed to her that the kings and
queens were making faces at her. She was losing every
game, signing IOUs with abandon. They were all turning
gray with fatigue, she thought, watching Mallory shuffle.
They would all just die right here and in the morning Mrs.
Mantessa would come clean them out of the room, toss
them onto the garbage cans like used-up rag dolls.

"I can't stand any more," Janet said abruptly. "I can't even see anymore. And I have to go to the bathroom."

"Okay," Hugh said. "Let's add up the IOUs and clear away the stuff." He added the figures, cashed in the chips, and announced the results. Regina had lost three hundred and ten dollars. She heard without caring. Janet had won a hundred dollars, and the rest had been spread around.

"Would you believe I've never played poker before in my life?" Regina said tiredly.

"Yes indeed," Conrad said, folding her IOU and putting it in his wallet. "Souvenir," he said. "When you're rich and famous, in a plush New York office with dozens of people waiting to see you, I'll use it for a calling card and gain instant admittance."

"Good game," Mallory said, standing and stretching. "Thanks, Hugh. You deal out at Vegas sometime or other?"

"Matter of fact that's how I earned college money," Hugh admitted. "Four years in a row I dealt during the summer months."

They talked about Las Vegas, and Janet turned to Regina. "I really do have to go to the bathroom. Would you mind going with me? If we stay together, maybe it's all right to use the one down here, not go upstairs at all."

The others fell silent at her words. Regina nodded. "We'll leave doors open all along the way," she said.

"I'll go with you and wait in the kitchen," Lucas said and his face darkened as he remembered that she had done that and he had thought she had arranged to be with Hugh.

Regina shook her head. "Let's not all separate."

"I'll go too," Mallory said. "I want coffee. I'll put it on while you and Janet are in the bathroom. Come on, let's get it over with."

He led the way through the hall, which was very still. He and Lucas paused at the kitchen door and watched the two women enter the bathroom. Then they went inside the kitchen and Mallory ran to the wall telephone and pulled the receiver down to his ear and started to dial the operator. He did not know the doctor's number and he never had looked up a number in the telephone book, did not know how to use it. There was buzzing static on the line and he jiggled the receiver several times and started to dial again.

"Who the hell you calling this time of night?" his father

demanded, jerking the phone away from him and hanging it up again.

"The doctor. Connie said Mother's sick, maybe dying." He wanted to add that Connie said their father was killing her, but he was afraid to. He knew about pregnancy and bleeding to death; just that spring one of the mares had died before the vet had got there. He had seen it, the pools of blood, the feeble attempts of the mare to raise her head, the long shuddering sigh . . .

His father slapped him so hard his head rang and his vision blurred. "Get upstairs to your room and don't come out again. You hear me!" He slapped him again and shoved him out into the hallway where Mallory reeled into the doorframe before he could balance himself. His father caught him and lifted him, slung him over his shoulder like a sack of potatoes and carried him upstairs, flung him down on his bed and left, slamming the door.

The next day he said they had no mother, as far as they were concerned Winona was dead and he never wanted to hear her name mentioned in that house. The day after that he had gone back to Washington and when he returned the following year he had a new wife and soon there was a new baby in the house, Janet. For days Mallory and Conrad had searched the grounds for a grave, and finally Mallory had decided that he had taken her body up into the mountains and heaved it over the side of a cliff where no one would ever find it.

He was sitting in his office in Washington studying the newest report concerning the extent of the black market activities when his secretary, Sally, came in with the special-delivery letter. The divorce was final. Winona expected the next three payments at thirty-day intervals . . .

She was gone, he thought. Really gone. Somehow he had believed she would change her mind, but she was out of his life, out of the boys' lives. It came over him like a crushing fist that he had loved her, that he still loved her. They would have made up again. They always had. Damn it, he loved her! That's why it had hurt so goddam much!

"Mr. Culbertson, are you all right? Can I get you anything?" Sally came around his desk to stand at his side; she reached out to touch him. "You're so tired. Let me take you home now."

He turned to her and she held him as long shudders passed through him. "They can't know," he mumbled.

"My God, I can't tell them their mother walked out." Sally held him and stroked his hair softly. Sally, the pretty Oregon girl he had met in Washington.

"Mallory! For God's sake, Mallory!" Lucas jerked his arm hard, forced him into a chair, and brought water. Mallory stared blindly, not responding, and in desperation Lucas slapped him and threw the water into his face.

Mallory seemed to collapse, to settle down into a pile of clothes and boneless flesh. He would have fallen from the chair if Lucas had not caught him and held him.

"I don't believe it," Mallory whispered finally, but he did. He knew it. Winona had abandoned them, had abandoned him. He put his head down on his arms at the table and wept as Lucas stood by him helplessly.

The bathroom was a large compartmented room, with one section that had the toilet and a washbowl, another with an oversized sunken tub and a wide window that looked out on the shaded patio. Steps went down to that part from the main section where there were two washbowls and a wide counter and two small, gilded chairs. Regina caught a glimpse of herself in the mirror and frowned. She had aged ten years since coming to this house, she thought, and turned her back on her image and opened the door to the tub compartment. From there he could see the hanging plants, the vines, the cool greenery that would be virtually unchanged year round. It was soothing to lie back soaking in warm water, and gaze at the soft world under the gray winter sky, watch mist gathering on the leaves, dropping in a glitter of light first here, then there.

The door to the sunroom opened and Greta came through, greeted him with her sweet smile. "You've had a hard evening. Come on, let me help you to bed."

"Promise," he whispered in his wavery voice. "Promise you won't let them take me to the hospital. I have to die in this house. Promise."

"Of course," she said, her voice as soothing as syrup.

"I told Strohm!" he cried. "He wrote it down in the contract. If I die in the hospital, you lose exactly half. Remember that!"

She nodded serenely, and he thought, he should have hired himself a wife back in the beginning, instead of trying to buy them one by one. She touched his arm—

"Regina! What happened? What's wrong with you?"

Janet shook her by the shoulders. Regina was slumped on the floor, propped up by the wall, her eyes open but blank.

She was slipping away, slipping away from the hands, toward a void. She yearned to be there, to be alone, forever out of reach, beyond Janet, beyond Greta, beyond Lucas, beyond everything, safe, to be nothing, a part of everything . . .

"Regina! Drink this!"

Janet held the glass of water to her lips, thinking: Not her! He can't want her! He hates women like her. He knows he can't trust her, she's too pretty, like Viola! "Please, Regina, snap out of it! Look at me! I can't leave you alone like this!" She wanted to cry out, "Leave her alone! Don't take her! It's not fair. I have the book!"

Regina was slipping further away, thinking this was how to recapture that moment on the mountain. Not in words after all, but like this, just giving in to it, letting it take over, yielding.

"Regina, don't move. I'm going to call Lucas and the others."

Lucas was sitting at the kitchen table with Mallory who still had his face pillowed on his arms. Lucas was under the plant table on the balcony, listening to his mother's voice screaming furiously at him. "Just stay and rot with your father! I don't care!" The front door shook the house as it slammed, and then he heard the tires squealing on the driveway. And he was thinking wearily that he was glad she was gone at last, and thinking that, Christ, he couldn't let her drive away in that state. She'd kill herself she was so blind drunk. Running for the truck, the air cool on his face, thinking, not the road, he'd never catch her on the road, but maybe he could if he crossed the field, shifting hard, heaving the wheel hard around, gunning it, and Lucas listening to the heavy noises, still hearing her last furious words: "I don't care!" Glad she was gone, glad she was leaving him alone . . .

He roared through the field and reached the road in time to see her flip over, hear the sickening sound of metal and concrete smashing together, hear the one shrill scream. How he hated that goddam bridge, had always hated that goddam bridge . . . He looked down and saw her looking up at him, her hair loose and flowing in the current of the river, running red away from her, her eyes staring at him

forever without blinking, without recognition, without seeing anything ever again.

Lucas shuddered and looked at Mallory and they were
standing across the living room from each other and Mallory was pointing his rifle and he said, "Just do it." He
meant it. He wanted to die, to be done with it all.

In the television room, Hugh concentrated on Regina,
slipping away, almost out of reach already. He called her
name softly, without sound, and he thought at her: "This
old man, he played eight, he played knickknack on my
gate. With a knickknack paddywhack, give the dog a bone,
this old man is coming home . . ." He was thinking at her,
Listen, Regina. Listen. And he continued the song, over
and over.

Regina thought, coming home, that was what it was like,
coming home. This old man is coming home. I'm coming
home. She resisted the song but it was in her head and
word by word it pulled her back, back from the void,
back to the bathroom floor.

"Thank God!" Janet breathed. "Can you take a sip of
water?"

Regina felt the water on her lips, singing in her head:
"This old man he played two, he played knickknack on my
shoe . . ."

Janet helped her stand up. She asked no questions; she
was afraid of the answers. In a moment or two they left
the bathroom together; Regina walked stiffly, as if she had
just come out of a very deep sleep. When they reached the
television room, it was as she knew it would be. Hugh was
sitting upright in a straight chair tapping his fingers on his
knees in rhythm to the song that was sounding in her
head.

Mallory and Lucas followed them inside the room and
silently they all began to arrange themselves for the rest
of the endless night.

No one slept although no one talked either. Janet saw
him coming at her again with the small quirt raised, felt it
hit, again, then again. "Filthy whoring cunt! No good
filth . . ." She wanted to cry out, to explain: "We didn't
do anything. We didn't do anything!" But she could only
scream in pain and fear. The words refused to come out
because they were a lie. They had done it, three times,
since her breasts had started to grow, and she had known

since the first time that punishment was due. She screamed and writhed and tried to die.

And Mallory stood looking at himself holding the rifle, thinking, not you, my first-born. God, just do it, do it and be done with it. Everything I touch dies, everything I love dies. Just do it.

Regina thought, a few sumacs over there at the edge of the firs to turn scarlet in the fall, a bright spot against the dark, and be soft green early in the year; visualizing it, not too many, three clumps maybe, no more than that. When the vision became too real she found herself singing the song under her breath: "He played knickknack all the time . . ."

Lucas dozed and woke with a start, listening intently. Hugh was sitting in an upright chair looking distant and remote, like a person in a trance, with only his fingers awake and active, tapping, tapping on his knees. Lucas strained to hear and shifted in the chair he was in. His legs twitched and he could no longer hold them still. And now his mouth felt as dry as his pocket, and as dusty. He tried to moisten his lips, his tongue was too dry. He could hardly swallow.

"What's wrong?" Regina asked, coming to his side, speaking in a soft voice in case any of the others were asleep.

"Thirsty. God, I'm thirsty. I've got to go get a drink of water."

"I'll come with you."

He hesitated, then nodded. All at once it seemed to be very clear to him, everything seemed so simple. From a distance he could hear his mother calling him over and over, searching the house a room at a time, calling his name.

He stood up and took Regina's hand. In his mind there was a picture of his mother's face, covered with water, her eyes wide open, looking up at him, her hair soft and fine streaming away from her. She was dead, he thought. She was dead. He heard her voice closer, and he and Regina left the room. He held her hand very tightly.

"Lucas, where are you? Don't you hide from me."

I won't, he answered. *Never again.* "Let's go upstairs," he said. "I have to have a bath. I'm grungy, and my leg is giving me fits. Warm water will help."

Regina nodded, but she was very pale, and inside she

was singing, "This old man, he played eight . . ." The house was quiet.

They went up slowly, with Lucas leaning on the rail all the way. In their room he pulled off his clothes and tossed them down on the foot of the bed while she watched, wanting to help, to do anything for him without knowing what she could do. He finished and stood before her naked, still too thin, and very young looking, boyish looking. He looked like a sick boy, she thought, and went to him, put her arms around him and held him fiercely.

"I love you," she whispered. "Oh, Lucas, I love you so much."

"I love you," he said softly and for a minute his hand smoothed her hair. "Don't cry," he said and leaned over to kiss her eyelids.

She blinked back the tears and he put her away from him and limped to the bathroom. "Do me a favor," he said without turning toward her. "In that drawer with the notebooks and junk there's one of my high school binders with some poetry in it, I'd like to show you, if you can find it while I take my bath."

She waited for the sound of running water and then sat down on the floor by the chest of drawers and started to pull out the notebooks, binders, sketch pads. His tenth grade science notebook was filled with meticulous drawings of crabs, a starfish, the skeleton of a bird . . . History notebook, decorated with unicorns and knights on armored horses. A castle that could have been a photograph. English notebook—pages of sentence diagrams, graded with red pencil, mostly D's, a few F's.

"I can't find it, Lucas. Are you sure it's in here?"

He did not answer and she glanced inside the drawer. There were still a few notebooks left. She picked up another one, and she heard: "Lucas, come on, we're leaving, honey." *This old man* "Lucas, don't you dare hide from me! Where are you?" *he played knickknack on my thumb* "You can't have him! He stays!" *with a knickknack* "Lucas, where are you? Come out right now!" *paddywhack give the dog a* "Just stay here and rot. I don't care!" *bone- thisoldmaniscominghome*

She was coming into the bedroom, looking, searching, calling.

"You can't have him!" Regina cried. Behind the woman the old man was entering the room.

"Leave him alone," he said hoarsely. "Just leave him alone!"

Lucas had to hide under the plant room table, Regina thought. He had to go there or she would find him. The woman opened the closet door, calling his name in a singsong manner. "Come on out, honey. We're leaving!"

"Go away! You can't have him. I won't let you!"

Now she looked at Regina, and moved toward her. "Is he in there? Are you hiding him?"

"Get out! Lucas, I need you! Tell her to go away!"

Lucas listened, and then said quietly, "I can't do that. If I'd gone with her . . . It's my fault, you see. If I'd gone, nothing would have happened. He didn't do it. I did. She knows it was my fault."

Regina was looking down at him in the tub where the water was already turning pink, and she braced against the door facing Viola, who was advancing, crooning to him now, calling softly.

"We'll be together. Just you and me. Come on, Lucas. Come out of there."

"You can't have him," Regina said desperately. "You already looked in there and didn't find him. You didn't find him anywhere!" The woman hesitated. Then she moved forward again and stretched out her pale hand.

If she went in there, Regina knew, she would join him in the water, comfort him, help guide the razor . . . She saw the river swirling away red, changing to pink, and Viola's face, her eyes open to the sky staring forever upward. "You belong in the river!" she cried. "Get out! Get back to the river!"

She took a step toward Viola who wavered but did not retreat. Regina looked past her at Culbertson. "Is this what you wanted? Stop her!"

He shook his head and Viola took a step forward, calling, "Are you in there?"

Regina screamed, and although it was wordless she was calling Hugh. She felt the doorknob cutting into her back; if she opened the door Viola could get in, she knew. But she could not enter with Regina there, she could not pass through her. The hand reached out closer and Regina screamed again, shrank back tighter against the door. She couldn't let that dead hand touch her . . .

The hallway door flew open and Hugh and Conrad ran into the room, past Regina, who dropped to the floor and curled up in front of the chest of drawers, both hands pressed hard over her ears.

In the bathroom, Conrad was thinking, Oh, God, he knows how. He grabbed Lucas by the armpit and hauled him up and out of the water. Hugh took his other arm and they swung him over the tub out to the floor. Blood was flowing from his left wrist, the cut was long, up and down, the right way to do it. He still clutched the razor blade in his other hand. He began to struggle, trying to wrench his arm loose, trying to get the blade up toward his own throat. Mallóry had entered by then and he hit Lucas once on the jaw and he went limp, the blade fell to the plush rug.

"Did he get the artery?" Mallory asked.

"I don't think so. He was just trying again when we grabbed him." They carried him, dripping water and blood, and put him on the bed. Conrad rushed back for a towel and began to dry him as Hugh examined the wound. Blood was flowing, but not in arterial gushes. "It just needs a couple of butterfly bandages, and then an overwrap," he said. Conrad nodded and hurried from the room. Hugh had finished drying Lucas by the time Conrad returned with the bandaging. He quickly and expertly bound up the wrist, and Lucas began to stir.

At the foot of the bed Mallory stood as if paralyzed by the sight of the blood, the wound, his thin young brother. Now he threw his head back and yelled, "You goddam bastard! Leave them alone! Leave them all alone!" His voice broke and turned into a sob, and he shuddered, helpless to make it all stop, helpless to undo any of the past.

The voices answered him, mocked him, swelling to a tumult. Regina had gotten to her feet without awareness; she had been standing out of the way, knowing they were doing everything, knowing she too was helpless. She closed her eyes. "Lucas, don't you dare hide from me . . ."

"Who the hell you calling this time of night?"

"Just do it!"

Inside her head she beard a quiet voice in a lilting rhythm: "He played knickknack up in heaven." She caught the line and continued it under her breath, mouthing the words: "With a knickknack paddywhack, give the dog a bone . . ." The voices subsided, were stilled. Lucas was moving feebly; at the foot of the bed Mallory was grasping the rail, bent nearly double, his eyes closed, and in the doorway Janet swayed, her hands hard on her ears, her lips compressed to a thin line.

"Where's his robe?" Hugh asked in a normal voice, breaking the spell. Regina picked it up from the other bed. She was vocalizing the words, hearing them, hearing them in Conrad's voice, and in Hugh's voice. Lucas groaned and started to sit up. Hugh got the robe on one arm and by then Lucas had his eyes wide open and was looking about in bewilderment. He remembered and looked at his wrist, neatly bandaged, and his face twitched in pain and frustration. "Why did you butt in?" he asked dully. "For the first time in my life I was going to do the right thing and you butted in."

"Viola isn't calling you now," Hugh said softly. "Look at me, Lucas. You were a little kid. You did what you had to do, and so did she. So did your father. None of you could have acted any differently. A little child can't be held responsible for the actions of an adult. What kind of universe would that be?"

Like Max and Wilberforce, Regina thought, and before her there yawned the same void she had wanted to fall into before, the same feeling of going home, of recapturing the moment on the mountain. She stretched out a hand, as if to feel the way, and she heard Hugh's voice, very sharp and hard, "Are you going to help? Or are you just going to stand there and shiver?"

She blinked fast, and the moment was gone.

"Put the robe on his other arm," Hugh ordered brusquely.

"Let's go down and make breakfast," Conrad said, taking Mallory by the arm. "I'll scramble eggs, make ham. Mallory, you're in charge of the juice and coffee. Janet, you still know how to make those biscuits?" He sounded grim, and he looked straight ahead, as if on all sides there were things he dared not admit to vision. Janet nodded, her cheeks wet, and Mallory allowed himself to be led out like a blind man. "Be ready in half an hour or so," Conrad said, going through the doorway.

"We'll be along in a minute," Hugh said.

Lucas stared at the floor, and now he started to get up. Hugh held him down gently and sat down by him. "Give yourself a little time," he said easily. "No rush."

Lucas felt his jaw. "You slug me?"

"I owed you one, remember?" Hugh said, taking the blame.

Protecting Mallory, Regina thought, and she knew it didn't matter. Hugh silenced her thoughts with a sharp glance.

"Luke, I want to make like a professional for a second. It's my job, you know. Look at it this way. Your father was a great artist, you all admit that. This place is as fine a work of art as anything that hangs in the Louvre. He was obsessed by beauty, creating beauty, and he needed the women around him to be as beautiful as the house they lived in, the grounds around that house. But they wouldn't hold still. It must have been fine at first to be that admired, but it was demanding them to be less than human to expect them to stay where he arranged them, the way the trees and the flowers stayed put. That's what he wanted, though. Of course they fought. And you were caught in the middle. Each of you in turn was caught in the middle. And you've been put through hell this week because of it."

"Why did he do this to us?" Lucas demanded. "That was inhuman. He was a monster."

"Probably. Most obsessed people are, in one way or another. I think he wanted you to know, each of you, that he wasn't as much of a monster as you thought. It's a terrible thing to think your father has killed your mother; I can't think of anything worse. He knew how bad it was, and I think he wanted to straighten that much out. He wanted you to know he was human, not very good much of the time, demanding and hard to get along with, but he wasn't a wife killer—not Winona, not Sally, not Viola— and in his own way he loved each of you."

Regina was standing near the foot of the bed watching them, listening to Hugh's soothing voice, his more soothing words, and she saw a ridge along his jaw that had not been there before. He was staring fixedly. His entire body looked as if he had been caught in the middle of a scream. How could he control his voice like that when he looked as if he were ready to erupt into pieces? She felt more afraid of him than of anything else she had seen or heard in the house. He had them all, she thought; he had gathered them all into himself and was one with them. He was containing them, controlling them because he was stronger than they were, because he knew them, understood them, knew how to make them obey him.

". . . his crutch?" He was looking at her, had spoken to her although she had not heard.

She drew back a step. His eyes were the eyes of a madman, glittery and inhuman. She fumbled on the floor for the crutch, not able to look away from him, as if now he held her also, knew how to force her obedience. She handed the crutch to Lucas and both men got up, Hugh steadying Lucas until he was firmly on his feet.

"You two go on down," he said and walked to the window, and stood with his back to them, looking outside. "Dawn's about to break," he said. "It's almost over now."

He had to clean up the mess, Regina thought, holding Lucas by the arm as they went to the door. She looked back; he was still by the window. They would kill him, she thought in confusion. No one could know that world well enough to control it and stay alive in this world. She didn't know what the thought meant. He turned and regarded her soberly for a moment; Lucas was moving ahead, and she hurried to stay with him.

Dawn came in silently with a soft rain that made the vines and trees and lawn sparkle. The house was still. As he had promised, Bill Strohm arrived at seven-thirty to read the will. Hugh met him at the door on his way out. For a few minutes he stood on the porch and regarded the farm, a work of art in four dimensions, changing with time, letting time itself finish it here and there, add a touch of silver, a patina of velvety moss. He took a deep breath and went to his car and left the property, driving slowly, feeling the road beneath his wheels, feeling the grasses growing, the trees stirring under the drops of water, feeling the freshening air as it moved through the ferns.

Bill Strohm waited until everyone was seated in the sunroom, before he opened the envelope he had taken from the safe in the master bedroom. There was a single sheet of paper. He adjusted his glasses and read it aloud:

"I, John Daniel Culbertson, declare that the test is officially over. Those who have gathered to hear this reading of my will have all passed the test. If you are winners or losers only you can tell. I direct my attorney, William S. Strohm, to proceed with the reading of my one and only will and testament, which he will find in my bedroom safe."

Strohm stopped reading. "What shit is all this?" he demanded furiously and strode from the room, leaving the paper on the table.

Conrad picked it up and read it silently.

"But what about the book?" Janet asked. "I have it. I thought he would want me to read something from it. Something . . ."

"You're the one? I wondered," Conrad murmured.

"And you're the one who tore up the place, I suppose," she snapped.

"No, not Connie. I did," Mallory said. "It was the only way I could make the voices stop." He sounded miserable.

Regina was slightly apart from the family members, watching them, hearing the silly song that sometimes dominated her thoughts, sometimes faded almost completely away. Nothing was explained, she thought, disappointed. He never tried to explain himself in life, and he would not have tried as a last gesture. It was out of character. She shifted uneasily in her chair and looked out the window. That was where she had been that day, looking in. He wouldn't have known how to make them understand him, even if it had occurred to him to try. He never understood a thing about people.

For a moment she was looking at her hand on the table, and it was Mallory's hand that she saw. And she knew that Mallory had the heaviest burden of guilt; he was the one who had chosen to believe his mother was dead rather than accept that she had abandoned her two boys, that she had been paid off. And from that belief the rest had sprung. Mallory looked pinched and exhausted. He would find Winona, if she was alive. He would take care of her, maybe settle her in this house again, if she wanted that. He looked at Conrad with so much pain etched into the lines of his face that Regina had to avert her gaze. But they would be all right, she realized; they would forgive each other.

She looked at Lucas and wanted to go to him, hold him hard, protect him from his own thoughts. He had to come to accept that his father would not have allowed him to leave that night with his mother. Culbertson had known where he was hiding; he had blocked the stairs when she would have gone up there. There was no way that Lucas could have prevented the crash; because he was blameless, he no longer had to blame his father. In time he would accept what he knew. Again and again Culbertson had tried to protect them, had shielded them from truth too painful to face and they had reviled and hated him for it.

The house was stirring again and she found herself singing under her breath.

Strohm reentered the room, red-faced and angry looking. "This is the original will I drew up for him," he said. "Let's get it over with."

The song drowned out his voice; she could hardly follow the words. The lump and the road were one, and the trees and the road and the lump, and the man inside . . . and the house that rose before him, and the furnishings, the file cabinet . . . The song was getting louder in her head, the words faster and faster, running together. She thought distantly that she was not certain which would be worse, to have it stop or to have it continue forever. She dreaded having it stop. In the file cabinet, behind the folders, was the gun Laura had insisted on having in the house. It felt cool and heavier than it looked. It was loaded.

Janet began to laugh hysterically and Mallory put his arms around her. Lucas grabbed Regina, nearly crying, too excited to speak, and she realized that they had inherited the farm equally.

"We won! We won!" Janet was crying. "We beat him!"

"It's over," Mallory's deep voice rumbled. "Thank God, it's over. We don't even have to stay here!"

"Perhaps if I ask Mrs. Mantessa to bring coffee we can settle down and finish this," Bill Strohm said, but no one paid any attention to him.

"Honey, it's over. I can feel it. Everything's stopped. It's really over!" Lucas was shaking her, and she thought he was crying, but he was laughing. "It's fucking over!"

. . . heplayedknickknackonmythigh . . . She was looking at Hugh sitting behind his desk holding the gun. The song stopped and there was a terrible silence in her head and she remembered his finger puppets, his falsetto: "As for you, Wilberforce, take that!" This is what Culbertson had wanted to give them, she thought. It could never be explained; it had to be experienced. He was so wrong about people always; he thought they could take it, that they could live knowing this. *Max and Wilberforce,* she whispered to Hugh, *that's the real legacy, isn't it?*

He looked at her without expression. "You don't have to know it," he said. "You can still reject it, forget all this. Get out and forget it, Regina. You don't have to know it."

"But I do know."

He shook his head. "Not yet." He looked past her at the glaciated mountain, dismissing her, recapturing a private moment. She watched him raise the gun, and she shared his eagerness as he pulled the trigger. For a moment she knew she was in the center, that she could choose which direction to take; for a moment she considered pain and humiliation and unhappiness, and for the same moment she considered love and joy and the incredible beauty of the world.

With the sound of the shot still in her ears, she slumped in Lucas's arms unbalancing him and together they fell to the rattan sofa. She heard her own voice in her head: And the farcical times, and the sad, and the ecstatic . . .

"Oh, for heaven's sake," Bill Strohm breathed.

"I'm all right," Regina said, trying to untangle herself from Lucas. "I got dizzy all at once."

"It's the excitement," Janet said, hovering over Regina and Lucas while Conrad helped Lucas to his feet. He sat down by Regina again immediately and put his arm around her.

"Can't you skip the rest of it?" Conrad asked Strohm. The attorney tightened his lips and Conrad said hurriedly, "Okay, okay. Read the goddam will. I'm going to get her some water."

He left and came back with a glass while Bill Strohm finished reading the will, racing through the words, the clauses. When he was done, he stood up and left without their noticing.

"Honey, it's okay. You're fine. You didn't eat a bit of breakfast, after all, and up all night. No wonder you got dizzy."

He's dead, she wanted to tell them, but she held the words back as Lucas murmured to her.

"What it means is that we'll have a nice apartment for now, and later on a house of our own. I'll have a studio and you'll have an office, and we'll go out to eat a couple of times a week. And we'll take good vacations now and then . . ."

There was something she had to remember, she thought, something she had learned that was important, that she should tell them. She tried to recall it, but Lucas's words were in her head and whatever it had been, it was beyond reach.

"It isn't going to change us, honey, just make things a little easier, a little better. You feeling okay now?"

She nodded.

"We'll leave as soon as you feel up to it. Get that motel room you talked about, rest, eat. Do it all."

It didn't matter, she wanted to tell him. The house was quiet now; it really was over. And yet, for a moment . . . She frowned, trying to remember something that eluded her.

"We have to talk about the house," Mallory said. "My kids have grown up on the desert, it's what they like, but I don't know. Sometimes I think I must have webbed feet after all."

Janet nodded. "Someone should live here. A house deteriorates so fast if it's left empty."

Regina leaned her head against Lucas and listened to them almost dreamily. The house was quiet again, but there was no ominous quality to the silence now, it was rather as if good manners had taken over, this was how a house should behave.

It was decided that Mallory would stay in the house, make frequent trips back to his ranch, and get the legalities straightened out. And they could all come back at Christmas and make real decisions then.

"Doesn't the heather bloom around Christmas?" Janet asked.

No one could remember, and Regina found herself nodding. That was how it should be, each one separate, protected by an invisible shield . . . She remembered what she had written in her notebook: We came separately and day by day that separateness was stripped away until there was no I, no you, no other. She no longer knew what she had meant by that. Culbertson had brought them back to make them all relive their past, to sort out the true memories from the false, to understand themselves. And they had done exactly that. And Hugh? She felt a small tremor in her stomach and pushed him out of her mind again. There was something she should remember about Hugh, but it was gone for now. Later it probably would come back. Something about a silly song, a mountain, something . . . She deliberately turned her thoughts to New York, to apartment hunting, the space they could now afford, the long life they had before them, together. She would forget all this week; with the thought she felt a rush of anxiety that made her feel like a child singing as she walked past a cemetery.

Lucas was talking about the kind of studio he had always wanted, and he was fingering the bandage on his wrist. It would take time, she thought, a long time, but the wrist would heal; together they would find all the small pieces of Lucas that had been blown apart this week, and together they would put them back in place. They had time enough. She concentrated on his words, nodding with him, denying the memory of a glaciated mountain, of being for a moment in the center, of choosing.